D0394942

THE
MONSTER VARIATIONS

THE
MONSTER
VARIATIONS

DANIEL KRAUS

DELACORTE PRESS

Copyright © 2009 by Daniel Kraus

All rights reserved. Published in the United States by Delacorte Press, an imprint of Random House Children's Books, a division of Random House, Inc., New York.

Delacorte Press is a registered trademark and the colophon is a trademark of Random House, Inc.

Visit us on the Web! www.randomhouse.com/teens
Educators and librarians, for a variety of teaching tools, visit us at www.randomhouse.com/teachers

Library of Congress Cataloging-in-Publication Data
Kraus, Daniel.
The monster variations / by Daniel Kraus.
p. cm.
Summary: On his way to State University, nineteen-year-old James runs into a former friend and is immersed in memories from the year they were twelve and learned that monsters exist in the world—and within themselves.
ISBN 978-0-385-73733-3 (trade)–ISBN 978-0-385-90659-3 (Gibraltar lib. bdg.)–ISBN 978-0-375-89264-6 (e-book) [1. Coming of age–Fiction. 2. Best friends–Fiction. 3. Friendship–Fiction. 4. Family problems–Fiction. 5. Amputees–Fiction. 6. People with disabilities–Fiction. 7. Fear–Fiction. 8. Death–Fiction.] I. Title.
PZ7.K8672Mon 2009
[Fic]–dc22
2008023967

The text of this book is set in 12-point Berthold Baskerville.
Book design by Angela Carlino
Printed in the United States of America
10 9 8 7 6 5 4 3 2 1
First Edition

Random House Children's Books supports the First Amendment and celebrates the right to read.

For Benjamin Huff

CONTENTS

THE
MONSTER VARIATIONS

NOW

Hit

Five more minutes and I'm gone.

This was all James was thinking as he muscled the wheel left and pulled the car across yellow lines, pocked cement, a sleet of gravel and dust. Five minutes and a tank of gas and he would be on the road—no more stops until he saw the university rise from the hills. Then these towns, all of them, would be behind him and his new life would begin. He might never come back.

But first, fuel. James was just thirty minutes outside of town, in an even smaller township made up of little more than one sleepy tavern, a scattering of silos reaching up from competing cornfields, and a single derelict gas station contaminating the leafy countryside. There had been filling stations back in his hometown, three of them, but he had wanted to get out of there as quickly as possible. James aimed his vehicle at the fuel pump. *These small towns,* he thought, tasting rust in the air and feeling the sting of burnt oil in his nostrils. *Goodbye to them forever.*

The tassel from his graduation cap swung from his rearview mirror, and as he rolled the car up next to the pump, it bounced and twirled, striking out the sunlight, then blinding him with it, as it had been doing since he had set out, as it had been doing ever since graduation. His friends hung their tassels from their rearviews, so he did as well, but all summer it had been a constant, dangling annoyance that would not quit reminding him of the town he was leaving and the bright future that everyone kept assuring him was waiting for him just up the road, just a few short hours away.

James struck the tassel with the back of his hand. It exploded into a pom-pom as cheery as the crowd of parents that had applauded when he had given his class's graduation speech two months ago. He'd taken his diploma on that stage and shaken the hand of a school superintendent he had never met before but who nonetheless gripped his palm and purred through clamped teeth, "We're all proud of you, son. Go get 'em up at State." James had nodded obediently and now regretted it. How much longer would he have to be obedient? How many more times would he do what his mother, his teachers, his classmates told him to do? *Not much longer,* he thought, glaring at the tassel. *Five more minutes and I'm gone.*

Getting out of town had been a nightmare. His parents, divorced but living just ten blocks from one another, had seen to that. After all the years of waiting, and after all he had been through, James thought getting to college would be as easy and as pleasant as getting into his car and driving there. He was wrong. It involved one hundred hours of strategy, toil, negation, inspiration. To his parents, the end of the world was tied up with one question: which of them would get to accompany James on the trip? His father, a hand clutching at what was left of his hair, explained slowly to his mother that James was a young man, moving into a dormitory full of other young men, and it was against nature to be brought into such a world by a woman. James winced—his father walked right into that one.

"Who brought him into this world in the first place?" his mother replied, her bottom teeth fretting against the old scar that slanted through the pink of her upper lip. "I've raised him," she said, keeping her voice as steady as she could. "Five years, me alone, in this house, cooking his food and hanging his laundry, and with whose help? No one's. And I didn't do it so I could pass him off to you like a football, so you could score the touchdown."

It was an apt comparison. James felt battered by these endless negotiations. But what else was life? You be quiet, you get a cookie. Sit still for church and we'll go out for burgers. As far as he could tell, only the stakes changed with age. So he sat calmly as they argued—he even smiled on occasion—while envisioning for the both of them a thousand gruesome deaths: hacksaws, stranglings, meat grinders, escapee elephants. The violence of these images used to surprise and shame him. Both feelings, he had discovered, wore off.

His father believed that life was math, ratios, fractions, all things at which he excelled, so his arguments towered over those of James's mother; they were masterpieces of logic more convoluted than the advanced-placement calculus tests James had recently aced. Given enough time, his father could prove that mankind descended from calico cats or that the West had won the Civil War. Yet this was one campaign he could not win. His ex-wife, James's mother, had one single, unassailable point, which she repeated with myopic persistence: "It's not fair."

What they really wanted was to have the final word, the opportunity to impart some divine piece of parental wisdom that would trump all that came before it. But if there actually was wisdom to impart, thought James, why had they both waited this long to hand it over? And if they were so wise, then why couldn't they come up with a way for the three of them to get along?

Revenge fantasies could get him only so far. It was time for action. James considered his options and just one made sense: he needed a clean break from the people and memories that surrounded him. So, one week before leaving, James woke up early, called his girlfriend, Clara, and dumped her. He started to feel guilty; he refocused and didn't back down. She cried and James timed it: ten minutes, not bad. For the past several months she'd been a nice enough girlfriend, but he'd really only miss their physical contact, and knew that beneath the perfunctory tears she felt the same. Clara went to a different school, as had his previous girlfriend, Jennifer, and the thing he liked best about the arrangement was that they were ignorant of his anesthetized daily life: the smiling boy scoring straight A's in a world without risk or danger. With Jennifer and Clara he had savored the intoxicants of nastiness, flavors he hadn't sampled since he was twelve. He could treat these girls badly, and had, because there was no social consequence at home or in school. It was wrong, he knew that, but he was not willing to give more of his heart than was necessary to keep a girl's interest—his heart, in fact, seemed lost somewhere in the past. At college no one would know him and he hoped this would further facilitate recklessness. Perhaps the imaginary pain he inflicted on everyone would no longer be necessary because there would be real pain, his included, instead of this numbness that stole his life's every second.

His talk with Clara emboldened him. He called up his dad and told him his decision about the trip: "Dad, I'm driving to college alone." Objections followed but James obscured them by imagining piano wire around the throat, knees knocked out with hammers. Then he went upstairs and politely told his mom the same thing. He could not bear to watch her summon the tears, so in his mind he covered her with honey and gave her over to an army of ants.

Just as the first tremble reached her lip, the phone rang. James excused himself and took a shower, hoping the noise of the water would drown out the accusations flying from his mom to his dad about how this was his fault, if only he was not so selfish, so arrogant. Their spilled blood, never there in the first place, swirled past James's toes down the drain.

Even the goodbyes had to be simultaneous. His parents stood in the driveway looking as pitiful as scorned children who, having misbehaved, were being left behind while their guardian went to the circus alone. His mother's hair, tied tight at the nape of her neck, seemed to be the only thing keeping her face from folding in on itself. She avoided histrionics, but only because the neighbors would overhear and she didn't want it getting around that she had been denied a rite of passage this crucial. His father did an even better job of burying his disgruntlement. It must have been hard for him, having been denied a four-hour car ride during which he could've bestowed uninterrupted advice about his favorite topic, college. But James had heard it all before. How to win the respect of professors, how to handle his alcohol, how to have fun with girls, and all while *keeping his eye on the donut, not the hole*. This had been a favorite phrase of his father's ever since James's childhood, and

James knew very well what made up the donut: the diploma, the lifelong buddies, the connections that would score him jobs. All other distractions, the noise of everyday life, just let it fall down the hole.

He issued hugs and drove away. *I won,* he thought as soon as his parents were out of sight, but he did not feel it. He was off to the college they wanted him to attend, the very place where they had met and fallen in love. When James had toured the campus it had crossed his mind that he might like it there, too, but his likes and dislikes seemed immaterial. His arrival at State would be just another entry in the scrapbook his mother had dutifully kept since he was a baby, overflowing with newspaper clippings and report cards and party invites and school programs. The scrapbook had long been an enemy. It seemed to him an already written biography filled with only successes, no failures—a record that no real person could live up to.

On the way out of town, he passed friends' houses and saw their cars missing from curbs, saw mothers standing strangely at windows and fathers pacing the lawn, looking for trouble. These days recent graduates were being lost to college with shocking regularity, the way young men must have vanished during war years. It was James's duty to go, and if his calling was to die in the field or return maimed, so be it. He drove the long way out of town to avoid running into any more familiar faces, but it did not help. Every landmark and intersection was haunted. He was low on fuel but there was no way he was stopping, not in this town, not with ghosts waiting for him everywhere.

So he stopped at this discolored gas station stranded in the middle of a cornfield. He would fill up and then drive until he was truly free. He turned off his car. Seconds later there was a bell clanging and a figure in stained overalls loping toward him, wiping his hands on a filthy scrap of rag. It was someone he recognized. He looked again. Yes, it was someone he knew. James found that he could not breathe; his breath was sucked away and replaced with combustible fumes. A single spark and he would be in flames, and here that spark came: it was not just someone he knew, it was Reggie.

Each giant step Reggie took seemed to James to take an entire year, and the days and months peeled away in seconds: one step, two steps, three years. James braced for collision. Reggie was huge, his shoulders a whole size broader than the blue uniform that clung too tight around his arms and chest. There were small triangles of blood on his knuckles and elbows, wounds that were salved by grease and dirt and left to harden. If not for the name sewn into the wrinkled work shirt, James might not have believed that this was the same boy he had grown up with, the same boy with whom he had played and laughed and—that summer when they were twelve—screamed.

James stumbled from the car, looked over the hood. He felt it, dry in his throat, stinging his eyes: panic. This meeting was bad luck, the worst imaginable, and with

Reggie's speed there were no paths to escape. Reggie stuffed the rag into the back pocket of his overalls, spit onto the sawdust that soaked up an oil spill, then leveled his dark eyes. Leaves skittered across the cement, bad engines wheezed and spun in the periphery. The recollection crawled over James's flesh like fire: a fight, this was a fight, remember? It started in a junkyard six years ago and still had not ended. Reggie stopped walking and squinted across the car, his face in shadow.

"Hey," said James. His heart raked itself across the sharp blades of his ribs.

Reggie sniffed, ran a hand across his forehead, replaced sweat with dirt.

"How you been?" James added. His own voice sounded strange to him, shrill and childish.

Reggie made two fists and locked them under his armpits.

"Nice goddamn car," Reggie said—and that voice, though deeper than the last time James had heard it, was as terrible and exciting as it had always been: dangerous, jubilant, and taunting. The last words James had shared with Reggie had been after school one day near the end of ninth grade, when they had both found themselves in the boys' room, James having just finished tennis practice and Reggie having just wasted an hour's worth of detention. It had been three years after all the blood, three years since the fight in the junkyard where they both should have thrown punches and hadn't. And there they were, alone, with enough hard surfaces to beat them to meaty pulps. But they had not fought that day. Instead, they had exchanged grunts, which banged off the urinals and sinks and mirrors but managed not to reach any ears. Then they had stepped around each other and Reggie had left the restroom. When tenth grade started up that fall, Reggie's face had not been among the crowd. The fight, yet again, went unfought.

Three more years and here was Reggie, having inexplicably grown to two times his previous size. James felt tiny before him. He always had, even back when he and Reggie and Willie all had been best friends, long before James began to compensate for that feeling of smallness by stacking up the achievements his parents pushed him toward: good grades, sports, the school newspaper, dating the nice girl from the right family—all fodder for the dreaded scrapbook. As he had continued through high school, he had kept focus on these activities but could not shake the memory of Reggie, lurking behind the school, hanging out in the parking lot, concealed in a cloud of cigarette smoke, laughing, maybe at him.

But not now, not here. James glanced at the tassel hanging from his mirror and tried to bury the flush of embarrassment. After all, he was the one leaving for a college education and Reggie was the one stuck working in some abysmal garage in some worthless town. James exhaled sharply, sent a murk of exhaust and oil from his lungs. There was a ring on Reggie's little finger, almost lost amid the mud and hair. A tattoo snaked out from one of his sleeves. This was the kind of kid James's dad warned him about, and maybe for once his dad was right. Yet there was nothing to fear here. James was Reggie's equal, if not his superior.

"Where you been? You live here?" James asked, and it came out loud, like a demand.

Reggie's chin, lightly dotted with hair, made a vague gesture. "Not far." He took another look at the car, saw the boxes of clothing stacked in the backseat. "Off to school. Let me guess. State? Keeping your eye on the donut?"

James had not expected this, but should have—it was a tactic Reggie had perfected as a child, a method of throwing you off guard before going in for the kill. James paused for a moment as the hot wind pushed a drop of sweat down his cheek.

"You remember the donut," James said carefully. He threw a glance at the corrosion all around them. "Lots of hole around here."

"I'm not sure how to take that, sounds kind of dirty," Reggie said. "How is the old donut man these days?"

"The same, mostly. Older."

"Your mom, too? Older?"

James nodded, but cautiously, unsure of where he was being led. "She's still a mom. Doing what moms do. She laughs a lot—" James stopped; he had not meant to say this, but now the truth of it struck him. She did laugh a lot in his presence, maybe too often, and for the first time he wondered why. This was followed by an unsettling new concern. Would she laugh at all now that he was gone?

"Huh," said Reggie. "You know, I don't know if I can remember my mom laughing, not once."

"She's here?" James took another look at the gas station: the sun-blasted truck tops, the flakes of old paint twitching in the wind. "I mean, you still live with her?"

Reggie took a moment, then nodded once. "Works down the road at the bar. She's older, too. Older than you might remember."

Images of Reggie's mother flashed through James's mind. Ms. Fielder—or Call-Me-Kay as he and Willie had been instructed—young and pretty and often asleep, smiling plenty but laughing only in dry, insincere coughs. It was impossible to imagine her aged and wrinkled, fit to play a proper mother at last.

A pickup truck pulled in at the opposite pump. Two boys, nearly twelve themselves, leapt from the bed, pushing, falling, one second hostility, the next camaraderie. They spilled onto the pavement, blackening knees, and shot past Reggie. James tore his eyes away from them: the little boys, for all of their bluster, were too young, had not yet begun to truly fight. He turned back to Reggie. "You graduate?"

Reggie laughed. To his surprise, James found himself laughing, too. He had forgotten how infectious the sound was, how energizing; immediately he wanted the laugh back. Reggie was trying to unnerve him. With a flare of dirty fingernails, Reggie threw his greasy rag at James. Too light, it landed on the roof of the car.

"Bite me," Reggie said, still laughing. "Yeah, I graduated. You wouldn't believe the kids here, they make me look halfway smart. I graduated. I mean, I have the piece of paper that says it. I didn't prance around onstage or anything."

"I did." James said it like a taunt.

"Course you did. You probably made a speech, too, I'd bet money." Reggie took another step closer, laid a hand on the car as if evaluating its worth. "What are you going to study?"

"I don't know."

"Well, what's your major?"

"I don't have one."

"Huh." Reggie drummed his fingers against the roof. "Then why are you going?"

The grin Reggie drew was large and disarming. Was it a friendly joke or the feint that preceded the first connecting blow? James opened his mouth to respond, but looking at Reggie made none of the available answers seem any good. He tried to return the grin and failed. Why *was* he going? Was it only to escape the scrapbook? Or was it all in hopes of bending those straight edges he had forged and refined throughout high school?

He was lost in this thought when the two little boys ran up to the car and stopped suddenly, holding one another, throwing one another away. The bolder of the two stared at James, then Reggie, and appeared ready to speak. But then the father shouted, and both of them turned on their heels and hurried back to the safety of the pickup, angry and delighted. In their absence was noise: hammering, men shouting, an engine choking, music forcing itself through the small tin holes of a radio, murmured jokes as wadded dollar bills passed through truck windows. It was a cycle of events that had nothing to do with James. He looked down at his car.

"Hey, none of my business." Reggie coughed. "Fill 'er up?"

"No," James said. "I can do it."

Reggie waved him off and moved with quick, forceful steps, and suddenly he was right there, stinking of oil and perspiration and reaching for the pump handle. James tried to grab it first and their fists rammed together—mental flashes of tree-house heroics, cemetery mud, knife blades, monstrous things. Finally, it felt good, and James wanted more, his muscles ached for it, the thrill of blood and dirt.

"Back off," Reggie grunted, and he leaned in, his shoulder knocking James aside. Those shoulders, that voice, those flashing eyes: James had to look down at his body to remind himself that he was not twelve, this was not that summer when too many people had died, and Reggie could not boss him around any longer. Instead, what James saw was his own clean shirt, his new slacks, those shoes that wouldn't last one day working in an environment like this one. He chanced a glance at Reggie, who stuffed the nozzle into the tank and started the gas

flow, *thump thump thump*. Reggie looked wild and un-
steady, as if the shoulder contact had also brought home
to him visions of their past contact: hands boosting feet
over fences, brilliant bloody noses, wonderful bruises.

They both felt the impact before it hit.

"You seen Willie lately?" It was Reggie who struck
first.

These were the terrible words James had both
yearned for and feared. He didn't want to think about
that summer—he had kept it from his mind for years and
it had gotten him this far, all the way out of town—and the
funny thing was, he felt certain Reggie didn't want to res-
urrect it either. But James needed to finish the fight, and
there was no other first punch to be thrown.

"Not in a long time," James lied, so close he could
feel the heat from Reggie's skin. "You?"

Reggie snorted. "Man, I don't have time for him anymore. He's not exactly the most exciting guy I know." He
blinked, aimed another strike. "Remember those weird
phrases he was always repeating?"

"Of course."

"Remember the tree house? I still have the scars all
over my legs."

"Me too."

"You remember the Monster?"

James felt his fingers curl into fists. Reggie's eyes
flicked downward at the movement. The fuel pounded
into the tank, *thump thump thump*. Behind Reggie, a car
squealed from the garage, a truck rumbled over to the

next set of pumps. *Thump thump thump.* Reggie saw dozens of trucks each day, James realized, and it was all too possible that one of them could be the truck that took that summer of their twelfth year and ruined it, and maybe ruined all three of them in the process—James, Reggie, and Willie. It was his heartbeat now: *thump thump thump.*

Reggie, as always, knew just what James was thinking. He lowered his voice and closed his eyes and said the final thing: "You remember the truck?"

THEN

I Smell Meat

Willie Van Allen's arm was gone. The truck that hit him escaped, silver and purring, and it swept up a gust that was almost refreshing. In the hazy afterburn he lay, his face blank as sand, white as foam.

Willie's arm, or what was left of it, was tamped into the dirt, now part of the old tar road along with stones and bugs and beer cans and scrub-grass. There was blood, but it had mixed with dirt, become mud. There was bone, too, but the bone dove beneath the mud like a tree root.

His left arm was gone, but his shoulder was still there,

seared dark from hundreds of hours of baseball–they called it junkball–played upon a diamond with a right field wall of rusty, abandoned dinosaurs called Chevy and Ford, and left and center walls of buildings so dilapidated that people had long since given up trying to live there. The serious play was in the summer, just eight short weeks away, but the boys could not wait and hit the field while their breath still hung visible in the air and their tentative scurries were marked by morning frost. Willie was too short and too little to be much good, but that was fine: the vacant square eyes of these buildings were the only audience.

But perhaps summer, and junkball, no longer mattered. His left arm was gone. His left shoulder was larger than before, as if the weight of the truck's tire had squashed the muscle from Willie's arm upward, like you might squeeze a tube of toothpaste. Willie himself did not move, but he could feel the compacted ball of flesh inside his shoulder squirm with each beat of his heart.

Willie lay half on the road, half on the barren shoulder, trying to remember what had happened. He had been walking home from the diamond, in a hurry because there was school tomorrow–still eight more weeks until summer, an infinity–along with Reggie Fielder and James Wahl and that bully Mel Herman. Willie's dad was supposed to have picked him up at the edge of the park, but he never showed up. Pretty soon the light began to fade. James stayed with him for a while, but eventually he left, too. Finally Willie began the long trek home. He barely remembered seeing the silver truck approach. He was busy thinking to himself, *How come Dad forgot me?* He remembered shuffling to the side of the road to let the truck pass.

Now the warm firelight of an April dusk sealed him to the tar with the glue of his own blood, which slid to the asphalt and pooled beneath him. The fabric of his T-shirt hardened to a crust. There was no sound, but Willie imagined a soft sizzle.

He began to fully wake. He blinked at a sky so red it looked bloody. The grass around him screamed with bugs. Slowly, he let his head loll to the side until his warm cheek felt the earth's skin. He saw his left hand. It was way, way over there, far, too far away. He thought about moving his fingers and then his fingers moved. But it must've been the breeze, because that hand was no longer connected to his body.

Then Willie began to *feel* again, and nails hammered one after another into his body, cold and fast, in places he could not predict: his forehead, his backbone, the webbing between his thumb and forefinger. His shoulder felt the worst. It was throbbing and itching like mad. There was also something wet pasting his hair to the back of his neck. Willie pretended it was gum. Mel Herman had thrown gum in his hair more than once and it took Willie's mom over an hour to scrape it all out.

The pressure in his shoulder was building. He looked

at it, for the first time really scared. From the way his shoulder bulged, Willie almost expected to see a glittering mound of cockroaches tumble out of it, chattering and excited to be free. Instead, he saw only an arrowhead of bone. Willie made a face, his first one: he scrunched up his nose, and a delicate treble note briefly dimpled the soft skin between his eyebrows. It *hurt*. His shoulder really *hurt*.

Willie decided to get up. It was the toughest decision he'd ever made. Would it hurt even more? Would all his guts come pouring out the hole where his arm used to be? He had to try, he had to make it to summer—injury, maybe even death, would be permissible then, but not now, not eight weeks away. He creased his forehead and tensed his neck, trying to yank his narrow wedge of a chest into action. His body didn't move. Willie felt like he was made of the same brittle twigs he saw on the ground all around him, and if he actually sat up, maybe his spine would snap.

Fear bubbled up in his belly, slid partway up his throat, and sat there. He moved his neck—just a little—to see over the top of his swollen shoulder. Beyond, he saw the scattered remnants of his arm, now little more than a purple stain on the road.

Willie panicked and started crying. Where in the world was his dad? He called out for help with such force that the acid in his throat splattered over his tongue and teeth. He jerked his head around, looking for somebody, or maybe a house, a telephone wire, anything, and the movement woke up the rest of his body and told him things he had not known. His other arm, the right one, was dislocated from its socket. A pebble was lodged inside his right ear. A bottle cap was planted deep into his left calf. Both of his shoes, pliant and worthless from the hundreds of hours of rain, creek water, and junkball dust, had been flung right off his feet. His head, at least, was all right, but he had a road burn on his neck—a deep, oval groove of mangled flesh.

Then his shoulder split open with a sound like ripping fabric. Willie Van Allen passed out, thinking just one thought. Summer, for him, would never come.

∗　∗　∗

But it did come. Proof was everywhere.

The wind could be seen; that's how fast it was. The grass could be heard; that's how green it was. He could smell laughter in the air, like melted waffle ice cream cones; that's how happy they were, all of them, everyone in town, in seed company hats and farmer's tans and dresses so new you could still see the dimples where they had hung all spring on store racks.

It was summer, finally summer, eight weeks later—he'd made it!—and the days, how perfectly terrible *hot* they were. Days like these made it practically a punishable crime to be a girl, and twelve-year-old boys everywhere were thrilled to be off the hook. The sun, everyone swore it, was closer that year and sagged lower, tickling tree leaves and roasting the skin of the three of them, Willie and Reggie and James, as they ran, which they were always doing—through infield dirt, playground blacktop, or scratchy, overgrown ditch weeds—arms pinwheeling and knee holes yawning ever wider; Willie in stripes, his arm stump still bandaged, James in something uncomfortable with buttons, and Reggie, as always, bringing up the rear.

Reggie was confident enough to let the other two go first, and often wore almost nothing at all, having already set his shirt on fire and thrown it into the pond, just for fun, and another time used one to catch a frog, and another one to wipe the caked soot from the windows of that creepy, abandoned shed, something he had been dying to do all winter—hell, for longer than any of the boys could remember. Willie had a theory: Reggie's mother—Ms. Fielder, Call-Me-Kay—must have spoken of that shed while Reggie still slept in her belly. Or that wonderful tire yard. Or that giant sewer pipe so big you could stand up in it. Or that spot beneath the railroad tracks where each passing train showered you with cool flakes of dirt and rust. Reggie's mother must have spoken of these places constantly, because Reggie somehow knew of them, or was drawn to them by a secret frequency inaudible to Willie and James. Reggie never got lost on the way to anywhere forbidden, not that Willie could tell, nor was he ever afraid.

"Martians will invade," he promised some afternoons. "And our families will be killed dead in their shoes."

The fair always came to town on the first week of summer, right after school let out, when the green lawn of the fairgrounds suddenly gave rise to tents, food trailers, and carnival rides. The men who worked the rides were beyond men. They were fatter than the boys' fathers (except Reggie, who had no father) and wore fuller beards and longer hair. Their forearms were thick and blue with illustrations and their hands smelled sharply of kerosene. Though Willie sensed that the men were less offended by his missing limb than normal people, they were also without pity. They stood with arms crossed and looked at the boys with something between amusement and murder.

The boys kept running.

"We will all marry girls," promised Reggie. "And we'll be there when they die."

They tried to pop two balloons with three darts and failed. They tried to toss one basketball through a hoop and failed. They tried to toss one plastic ring around one soda bottle—*any* bottle, come *on*. Willie's face was sticky with cotton candy because he didn't have a second arm to pull off the wispy remainders. James emptied his pockets to buy a one-dollar mirror etched with the contour of a sexy lady, but later gave it to Reggie, conceding that his own parents would never allow something so lewd and impractical inside a house already sparkling with three floors of clean, inoffensive mirrors. The Wahls' housekeeper, Louise, was directed to clean all of the mirrors weekly, and the floors and windows and light switches, too. James claimed that he found this routine needlessly thorough, but Willie and Reggie had both caught him staring intently into the mirrors as if searching for some kind of barely camouflaged flaw. Sometimes he would press his thumbnail into his upper lip for a full minute and then remove it, and show the temporary white slash to one of his friends. "Look," he'd say, "I have a scar there, just like my mom." It was unclear to Willie why James would want such a thing, or why he'd go through so much pain to keep it for only a few seconds.

At the top of the Ferris wheel they sat together and rocked as someone, miles below, got off. Reggie pointed to the lights at the edge of town and with a whoosh of breath tried to blow them out like candles. James announced that he wanted to be a baseball player when he grew up, but that it would never happen because he was too skinny. Willie asked James what kind of car his parents drove, because his mom wanted one just like it but said it was too expensive. One day, predicted Reggie, he would be a famous criminal or famous cop, either one was okay with him. James said he'd be the cop who caught Reggie the robber, or the robber who evaded his cop, and their gunfights would go down in history. Willie asked if either of them knew of any good jobs for his dad, because he'd just been fired—he was good at selling things, maybe he could sell toys or sports equipment? Reggie tapped a finger on the car's railing and said *this,* this very moment, was perfect because they were so high up that no one below could see them, and as far as anyone knew there could be anyone in this car: men, legends, ghosts, monsters.

When the sun dipped just below the trees, Reggie and James turned bright orange and their eyes flashed like those of African tigers. Willie wondered if he looked that way, too, and now wished he had the sexy-lady mirror so he could see. The boys smiled, but with closed lips. They measured each other's reactions, then tested them by saying things that were mean and confusing. They spit and squatted in the dust like carnival men and acted as if they knew all about life and death—and maybe Willie knew about death, just a little.

It had been at a golden hour just like this one, three weeks ago, with Willie recently freed from the hospital and his mother's side and reintroduced to the land of the living, that Reggie had made the three of them join as blood brothers, cutting their palms with an old buck knife and holding them together while they all looked at their feet, suddenly shy.

"I'd give anything to be old," Reggie had said that day, his voice hoarse, watching the dark red liquid roll down the last middle finger Willie had.

Against all odds, night came. There was a man picking up trash with a poker. The rides lost their blinking lights. Reggie kicked the dirt, unhappy. James mumbled about his parents and how they'd warned him to be home hours ago, how they were probably already on the phone trying to find him. Willie, meanwhile, sat and watched his two friends, taller and bolder and better-looking than he, and with two arms each. But instead of being jealous Willie was only glad. It was summer, he had made it after all, and any new pain he felt certain he could swallow whole.

Where All Jokers Must Make a Jump

A kid was dead. It was a kid James and Reggie and Willie knew from school, a pudgy sixth grader with a florid complexion named Greg Johnson. Greg had been run over by a truck around eight-thirty a few nights ago, right after buying a soda at a corner store. None of the witnesses recalled the make, model, or color of the vehicle, but nevertheless swore that the truck never slowed down. It ran over Greg Johnson like he was made of paper. Grown-ups were calling the event a "hit-and-run." What worried everyone was that it had only been nine weeks since Willie Van Allen had lost his arm.

Last night there had been a big meeting. It was a small town and when two kids got hit by trucks, this apparently was what grown-ups did. Naturally the Van Allen parents had attended and so had James Wahl's folks. Reggie Fielder's mom, a waitress, was working that night, so Reggie relied on James and Willie to relay the details.

But there was only one detail that mattered, according to James. There was going to be a curfew. No kids on the street after eight p.m., effective immediately. "For how long?" Reggie asked James, who had begged the same question of his dad: "For how long?" James's dad only shrugged, took a pen from where several sat leaking into his shirt pocket, and busied himself with the columns of numbers that made up his work. "As long as it takes," he said.

The boys agreed it was terrible news. The summer wasn't totally ruined, but close. After all, eight o'clock on a summer night wasn't even *night,* it was the same as daytime only better—dimmer, cooler, and veiled. Now they'd have to withstand the stuffy interior of three separate houses several blocks apart from one another, and all because some guy was zooming around town looking for twelve-year-old boys to run over?

It's not fair, James thought as he pressed his forehead against the van window. The world beyond was stone gray and moved too fast to understand. Anything could mean anything. There was an old man scolding a dog—maybe he did sick things to children. There was a tall man brushing himself off in front of a barber pole—maybe he was a drunk, maybe he beat his wife with a wooden spoon. There was a little troll-like woman hobbling her way down the sidewalk—who knew, maybe she liked to run over kids in her silver truck.

It was a bad day to go anywhere, and James was headed for a funeral. There had been a wake the night before—this, he had learned, was when everyone filed by the casket to get a peek at the dead person. He was not allowed to go and was too scared anyway. Willie's parents did not allow him to go either; ever since the second hit-and-run, the Van Allens had become even more protective of their son. Reggie, of course, went to the wake, and because his mother worked nights he did it alone. James didn't know how Reggie got so brave, but Reggie was determined to see a dead kid, and if the funeral home had sold tickets, he would've arrived early to get a good seat. Reggie owned no dress clothes, but borrowed one of his mother's white button-down blouses and tucked so much fabric into his pants it looked like he was wearing diapers. He owned only white sweat socks, but soon enough found a black marker and went to work.

After the wake, Reggie had come knocking at James's bedroom window. It was easy to do: if the family van was parked in the driveway alongside the house, Reggie had only to scale it, leap onto the lower roof of the three-story split-level home, dart across the shingles, then tap on James's windowpane. Before the accident Willie also used to do it, but these days he had to use the door.

According to Reggie, Greg Johnson was definitely dead. Three people took the podium to speak. There were twenty huge bouquets of flowers, and more Styrofoam cups of coffee than Reggie had ever seen. Four people left during Mr. Johnson's emotional plea to find the killer. Eleven people cried. Twelve people hugged Reggie, despite the fact that he didn't recognize any of them, aside from Mrs. Van Allen. By the time it was all over, his socks were almost white again, and Reggie guessed it was all those damn teardrops that did it.

"What did he look like?" James asked.

"He looked pretty good" was the response, but looking was not enough, not for an opportunist like Reggie. He hung back to the very end of the viewing line—at least, that was what he told James—and then leaned his elbows on Greg's casket, settling his chin against the cold, new metal.

"There was something weird with his eyes," Reggie reported. "I'm not kidding. There was something all wrong with them." When asked to explain, Reggie would only hint that the protuberance of Greg's eyelids was somehow unnatural, either too big or too small, perhaps hiding objects that were not Greg Johnson's eyeballs at all, but artificial glass that the mortician inserted after scooping out the originals—or, maybe, after the original eyeballs had been knocked out by the truck that struck Greg in the back. James imagined something terrible: one of Greg's eyeballs mashed beneath a truck wheel, and the other eyeball carried away by an industrious

34

squirrel. James wished his brain didn't think of things like this, but he couldn't help it.

"I couldn't reach it," Reggie said, "but there was something in Greg's hair, near the back, back here." Reggie touched his head where fathers got bald spots. "I thought it was beads. You know, like religious beads, but why would there be beads in his hair? Then I thought bugs. I thought they were ticks, maybe feeding on him." Reggie spoke calmly in order to shock James. It worked. Reggie shrugged. "But I think it was some kind of stitches. Big huge stitches. Or maybe staples. To keep his head shut."

Then there had been motion in James's house—heavy footsteps on the spiral staircase, drawers banging shut, the squeak of the medicine cabinet. James's parents, both of them, were coming to his room, clutching stiff penny loafers and a tie for the funeral, so instantly Reggie vanished through the window, lowering himself onto the van roof before disappearing into the dandelions.

And now here was James, his hair dull, his face nervous and ashy, feeling in his bones each pebble that passed beneath the van's tires. He was off to the funeral, his first, and he felt sick. He hoped Reggie wouldn't be there because then James would have to hide his sick feeling. But he knew Reggie would show up, even without his mother, who inevitably would be working the lunch crowd—Reggie wouldn't miss this for the world. "You're chicken," Reggie would say if James skipped the funeral, and he would be right.

The van turned and a cemetery mausoleum suddenly leapt into the sky, then Jesus on a cross. Then, rising like an army, tombstones, hundreds of them. James read the names: Smith, Kaufman, Brown. No Johnson that James could see, and for a moment he hoped it was all a mistake. He looked harder. Even through the grayness of the day the grass in the cemetery was too green. He wondered why and felt even sicker.

Through the van window he saw a blue tarpaulin stretched over maybe two dozen metal folding chairs. The tarp snapped loudly in the irritable gusts. James looked up. The clouds were like wet paper sacks–rain threatened to soak right through. There were already people congregated, all of them glancing at the sky, holding black umbrellas at their sides, murmuring to each other and offering small handshakes. It looked to James like these handshaking grown-ups were inviting each other into the fresh dirt hole at their feet.

Staring up at the casket was Reggie, looking small and pale next to all the grown-ups in black. Willie would not be attending. As James's parents had cinched a tie around his neck and stuffed away a rogue shirttail, they had said that the funeral would be too emotional for Willie, who was already such a delicate child even before all this terrible stuff happened, before he got that ugly puckered scar on his neck, before his mangled shoulder had to be softly snuggled inside a safety-pinned shirt sleeve every single morning. Later, James reported his parents' observations to Reggie, and while Reggie did not agree that Willie was all that sensitive, he did concur that it was smart to keep him away. According to Reggie, if the grown-ups at the funeral saw Willie's stump it might be like the wake all over again, only worse–this time people would be crying right out in the open.

The van stopped. Doors were opened and dry air swept in. James felt a puff of wind peel his forehead from the glass. He was outside. His butt was in an uncomfortable metal chair next to Reggie. And there was Greg Johnson's casket, kid-sized, as silver as the truck that probably hit him, latched shut and already striped with bird dung. The kid was dead. His back snapped like a stick. His eyes popped out. His head shredded against concrete.

He had died fast. Or so they said.

The funeral service was short. A man read scripture. The sun emerged from clouds and the shadows of the tombstones reached for the mourners, yet no one ran. One of the shadows fell on James and he felt his heart yanked. It made him want to vomit, and when that feeling passed a whole bucket of tears filled his eyes. He tried to hide them. He didn't want Reggie to see. He didn't know why he was crying. He barely knew the kid. He took a deep breath, smelled soil, and wondered if Greg's obituary would end up in that scrapbook his mom kept, or if one day his own death notice–JAMES WAHL, DECEASED–would find its way into the pages.

Four men stood to put Greg Johnson in the dirt. The coffin was lowered on thick straps connected to some sort of pulley, and it shuddered like it was too heavy and filled with wet laundry, old rags. James wiped his eyes—it *was* filled with old rags, it *was*. One corner of the coffin dipped too fast. Men's arms trembled at the weight, and they leaned backward to correct the mistake. James caught his breath, certain that the casket would tip and Greg would spill out, his staples undone, the loose skin of his head flapping. The men fought for control. Their shoulders curved inward and their muscles clenched. But the weight was too much because it was death, and eventually it took everyone down.

Kids (Poor Creatures) Often Fight Good Sense

Reggie lay on the roof of James's house for a long time. He thought about his own house and how you could fit the entire thing inside of James's living room, but how it was still better than his previous two homes, both short-lived experiments crowding him into the spare room of one of his mom's now ex-boyfriends' houses. He watched as the Wahls' housekeeper, Louise, left for the evening, perhaps tired of waiting. Reggie had known Louise most of his life and loved her dark humor and vivacious demeanor—but he could outwait her any day of the week. He listened as the ancient grandfather clock in

Mr. Wahl's den tolled six, then seven. It was no different than holding air under water: if he took slow, even breaths and did not move an inch he could remain in this state all night. He had done it before.

Finally he heard the Wahls come home. He kept breathing, in, out. He smelled cooking meat and tasted bread and green vegetables in the air. He heard china plates being set for dinner. Chairs clopped and squealed to meet the table. Glasses sang, silverware spat. He waited.

Reggie had no brothers or sisters and his father was in prison. His mother worked most days and nights at a restaurant—according to her, this was still not considered "full-time," though this baffled him—and so rarely did they dine together. Instead, she brought home food and Reggie would reheat it and eat alone in front of the TV, between bites bending the antenna to steady the wobbling picture. Reggie was usually envious of the dinnertime James enjoyed—Louise's feasts spread across that spacious, gleaming table beneath that glittering chandelier—as well as the conversations his family shared, discussing world news and the stock market, grilling James about his homework and friends, repeating to him the importance of establishing a good routine that would carry him through into college: *Keep your eye on the donut, not the hole.* But not tonight. Tonight Reggie was glad to be alone. He cracked open the window so he could catch the after-dinner conversation.

Mr. Wahl's voice was too low-pitched to cut through

the drone of the air-conditioning units and James's mother wasn't speaking. Only James himself could be heard. Reggie closed his eyes and listened.

"I'm fine."

"I'm *normal*. I'm fine."

"Yeah."

"Yeah."

"I know."

"I *know*."

"I don't know. Not really."

"Some. I knew him a little."

"I don't know where. Maybe from the playground?"

"Yeah. Sometimes. But usually he played by himself. He was just some kid."

"Willie? I don't know. Maybe. I don't know. You'd have to ask him."

"Of course I know: Willie got hit by a truck."

"No, it was a truck. A silver truck."

"Because Willie *said* it was a truck."

"Because he *said* it was silver."

"I won't."

"I don't go on those roads."

"I don't go on those roads *any*way."

"Dad, I stick to the *main* roads."

"I don't."

"I won't."

"Reggie? How come?"

"He's not."

"He's *not*. It was just that once. Reggie never usually hits *any*body."

"He's fine."

"Reggie's fine, Dad."

"He doesn't. I mean it. I do what I wanna do. Reggie doesn't make me do anything. I do what I say."

"Okay."

"Okay."

"Fine, I'll tell him."

"I'll tell him what you said."

"Fine."

"Fine."

"Fine."

"No. I'm not hungry."

"No, *thank you*."

There was some silence, then soft footfalls up the stairs. The door opened in James's room, then shut. Reggie counted to fifty before rolling through the window. He put on a smile.

"Hey," said James, flopping onto his tangled bedspread. His hand blindly reached beneath the twisted sheets and came up with his baseball cap. He crammed it over his neatly combed hair and relaxed. His hand played along the edge of the bill, which was soiled with years of dirt and sweat and summer.

"They asked me a hundred questions," said James. "I didn't think it was ever going to end. I'm starving, you got anything?"

"Me? I was counting on you," said Reggie.

42

"Nuh-uh."

"Well, crap."

They said nothing for a moment and the silence felt different than ever before.

"Tell me what?" Reggie asked.

"Huh?"

"You told your dad you would tell me something."

"Oh, right."

James paused and looked around his room. He was suddenly embarrassed by the room's size—in comparison, Reggie's room was a closet—as well as the amount of little-kid toys scattered about. Reggie had long ago pawned his army men and building blocks for pocket change.

"He says we shouldn't hang out so much," James said.

"Huh."

"I mean, he always says that."

"Right."

"He says especially at night. Especially at night we're not supposed to hang out so much."

"No kidding."

"It's not that he doesn't like you," James said. "He likes you okay. Seriously. It's just for some reason, he thinks you . . . I mean, I don't really know what he thinks. But don't worry about it, okay? I don't care what he says. I mean, you know. It's *summer*."

James shrugged and looked away. He felt small and restless beneath Reggie's patient gaze. James fidgeted with his cap and looked out the open window.

After a moment, he spoke again. "Have you really thought about it? I mean, him being dead?"

With a long, quick arm, Reggie punched James in the shoulder. James recoiled—Reggie always hit a little too hard—and remembered his father's comment about Reggie's aggression. Sure, there had been some incident at school where Reggie had punched a kid. So what? It had been one incident among many. Lots of kids hit lots of kids. James couldn't figure out why his father always singled out Reggie.

"Don't say another word," said Reggie as James lifted defensive fists.

"Ow."

"We can't talk about this dead stuff without Willie," said Reggie.

"How come?"

Reggie smiled, but there was something in the expression that James did not like. He said, "You'll see."

* * *

By the time they reached Willie's house it was almost seven. James couldn't believe it: in one hour it would be illegal to be outdoors.

Normally the boys would have met in Willie's tree house. It was right beside his home, nestled within tall, strong branches. Built by Willie's father, it was unusually formidable, big enough for three boys to lie down in sleeping bags and spend the night, which they had done many times over previous summers. Now when Reggie and James looked at the tree house it was different, and James knew why. It was because Willie would never again reach it. For a second, James's eyes felt funny, like he might cry, but he coughed and made the feeling go away.

They knocked on the door, and after a while Mr. Van Allen's face appeared. After searching above their heads as if expecting a cadre of police officers instead of two twelve-year-old boys, he looked down at them and his expression changed to one of muted pain. Ever since Willie's accident, Mr. Van Allen seemed disoriented, as if he never knew exactly how he'd found himself standing there at the front door. As dads went, James had always figured Mr. Van Allen was all right, even though he had spent most of his leisure time within a nest of magazines, playing cards, and televised sports, making occasional loud offers to fetch James a can of beer. James had always assumed these offers were jokes, but nevertheless they had made him uncomfortable.

But that Mr. Van Allen, as intimidating as he had been, was preferable to the unkempt, plodding automaton whose face they only ever saw on the other side of a screen door. Mr. Van Allen had just a little bit of hair around the sides of his head, and these days it stood up in wiry twists. His eyes were red and the skin around them was blue, and it looked like his sockets were sinking slowly into his skull. Mr. Van Allen had always smelled of beer, but now smelled like he bathed in it. He still smiled when he spoke, but his smiles made James and Reggie nervous.

"Willie's upstairs, boys," he said, thumbing open the door lock.

"Thanks, Mr. Van Allen," they said, and ran past him as fast as they could.

Willie's house was nowhere as big as James's—few houses in town were—but it was bigger than Reggie's, and done up nicer. Still there was something about it that felt phony to James, as if the entire home was a scaffold dressed with fancy ornaments that, if you looked close, were not very fancy at all. It smelled harsh, like cleaning chemicals, and was always too hot. James and Reggie hurried to Willie's room, where they could open a window to escape the suffocation.

It was strange to have a friend with only one arm. For two weeks after the accident, they weren't allowed to see Willie. As usual, Reggie had acted like he knew everything. "He could die at any moment," Reggie had said for over a week. When that proved false, Reggie started saying, "There could be permanent brain damage, you know. He might not be able to talk. Maybe spit will just come pouring out of his mouth whenever he tries."

But when Willie had returned home from the hospital, he seemed fine. His skin was paler than before and his hair longer, but he had on a great big grin and brand-new baseball cap. The main difference was that where his left arm used to be was now just a little lump, though it was always hidden inside a sleeve fastened shut with two safety pins. James and Reggie had still never seen it.

They had been allowed to stay only a few minutes that first time—Mrs. Van Allen had shooed them out, flapping her hands and laughing. Unlike her husband, Mrs. Van Allen had grown cheerier following her son's accident, though this too troubled James. Why was she working so hard to convince them that everything was wonderful when the contrary evidence was right there in Willie's stump?

A couple of weeks later Willie was back running around with James and Reggie, almost like normal. Only now his missing arm caused a curious imbalance, and at seemingly random moments he would holler and fall on his face. He couldn't play junkball anymore, but actually it worked out perfectly: the boys had always wanted an umpire and Willie had always been the worst player. It wasn't all his fault—he was the shortest kid in sixth grade and one of the skinniest, too. The problems continued from there. His ears stuck out and he had a long nose. Even his teeth were screwed up—the metal braces he wore weren't scheduled to come off for three more years. Willie said the braces were going to "scrunch up his teeth." James thought it sounded like a good idea because each of Willie's teeth was about a mile away from the next, and sometimes globs of food would settle in these spaces until Reggie noticed it, groaned in disgust, and demanded Willie go rinse out his mouth.

When they got upstairs, Willie insisted on hearing about the funeral. He listened with huge eyes and absently scratched the scar on his neck, which wasn't wet but always looked it.

"What are they going to do with Greg's drawings?" asked Willie.

"His what?" asked James.

"His drawings. On the walls outside the art room, with everyone else's. Are they just going to throw them away or what?"

"Forget his stupid drawings," said Reggie. "I want his shoes. He had cool-as-hell shoes. You think his family will give all his stuff away? Or hold a big sale?"

"I keep thinking of where he stood in line for gym," Willie said quietly. He nodded his head like he approved of the memory.

"What about his locker?" asked James. "I bet he left tons of stuff in his locker."

"Right," said Reggie, his eyes lighting up. "Crap, man, there might be *baseball* cards in there."

"In gym, Greg Johnson—walking around in blue shorts," said Willie. James ignored the comment. He was used to Willie's fantasies. Secretly, James wondered if this was how Willie got hit by the truck. Isn't it possible that Willie had been daydreaming again and wandered into the middle of the road?

"He sucked in gym," said Reggie. "The guy couldn't catch a stupid pop-up. You ever see that kid try and catch a ball? It was embarrassing."

There was silence for a moment. The boys squirmed.

Finally Reggie sighed. "There's something I got to tell you guys."

James and Willie looked at him.

Reggie paused mysteriously, then spoke. "This could be our last summer."

James looked at Willie, then wished he hadn't. Willie's face was pink and vulnerable and his arm stump was tiny and useless. Something in James's stomach rolled nervously and he knew immediately what Reggie was talking about. Maybe they were next.

"But the curfew," James protested.

"But the curfew," Reggie mimicked. "What about the stupid curfew? Are we going to stay in our rooms every damn night and let the entire summer go by?"

It was a challenge, maybe a threat. James looked at Willie; Willie looked at Reggie.

"No?" Willie asked.

"That's right," said Reggie. "I know I'm not."

"Yeah, but your mom's not home at night, it's easier for you to sneak out," said James. "I got a mom and a dad, and now they got Louise on my back, too."

Reggie ignored the remark. "Look. Willie got hit in the daytime."

"Dusk, technically," Willie said. He shrugged when Reggie glared at him.

"All right, fine," Reggie continued. "But it was still light out. Now, Greg Johnson, he got hit at night. That means going inside at eight won't help because it could happen to any of us at any time and there's nothing we can do to stop it, except run real fast if we see a silver truck coming. What, you guys want to just sit inside and get old? Not me. We have to get out there every night, this summer more than ever. Because—and I'm not trying to scare you here. But because this could be our last chance."

There was some truth in what Reggie was saying, and also some silly drama. But James couldn't help it, he found himself nodding along.

"We should do everything we ever wanted to do," said Reggie. "We shouldn't follow any stupid rules. We should—"

"Take risks," Willie finished. James looked at Willie, alarmed.

Reggie nodded, and allowed himself a small smile.

"Now," he said. "I know there's stuff we've talked about doing but were too scared. I been thinking about this. All day I been thinking. James: you used to talk about climbing the fence and getting in the old swimming pool."

"Yeah, but that was forever ago—"

"And Willie, you used to talk about wanting to get on the roof of the MacArthur Building and see how far you could see. Remember? You used to yap about it all the damn time."

Willie was nodding dreamily.

Reggie grinned with so many teeth that James felt his own face grin in return. He hated himself for it; this reaction was just what Reggie wanted. Conversations like these were like fighting without fists, and James didn't know how he was supposed to fight back. It was too late anyway—by now Willie was grinning, too, and nodding to himself, his arm stump twitching like some kind of newborn animal.

James couldn't bear it anymore, he had to know.

"What about you? What do you want to do?"

Reggie laughed.

"The school, dummy," he said. "I want to hide out and spend the night at the school."

Everyone Just Leaves

It was true. Reggie had wanted to hide out in the school for years. It had started one day when they were sitting together under the slide at recess eating candy from a paper bag, the chill of an early autumn snaking down their backs, and Reggie saw smoke coughing from a school chimney.

"I never noticed a chimney," he said.

A few days later, while the class single-filed to the art room, Reggie overheard a conversation about the teachers' lounge.

"I never knew there was a lounge," he said.

The following week at lunch Reggie paused to get an earful of a custodian's exchange with a teacher. The custodian was holding a box full of props left over from a Columbus Day play the fourth graders had performed for the school. Moments later, Reggie slid his tray down between James and Willie, his eyes shifting and lit.

"Somewhere in this school is a costume room," he said.

Soon Reggie had sketched an impressive mental map of an alternate Polk Elementary, one with secret passageways and underworld chambers. Wouldn't it be cool, Reggie said on repeated occasions, to hide somewhere inside the school, wait until all the teachers and custodians had gone home, and then go exploring in the night? They could scream and yell as loud as they wanted. They could read private student records. They could bounce kickballs off the principal's door. They could *roller-skate*.

It was summer, of course, and school was out. But that didn't stop Reggie. Last year he had neglected to hand in dozens of assignments and was forced to suffer summer school, a strange daily ritual that Reggie described to his two friends as "just like normal school, except hardly anyone's there, and you can get as many questions wrong as you want because the teacher just wants to go home." Summer school had lasted for six weeks and, though Reggie had hated it, it had given him deeper insight into teachers. "Teachers are just like us," he explained. "They hate school, too."

Neither James nor Willie hated school, but they'd

nodded anyway. It was better not to get in Reggie's way when he was caught up in one of his schemes. If you did, he was likely to turn against you, attack you for being too wimpy, a little girl unworthy of being included in his plan. He might hate you for days, even weeks. So James played along, but reflected how strange it was that Reggie was finally excited about school, only now for all the wrong reasons.

With a vigor he never applied to his schoolwork, Reggie compiled a long, detailed catalog of all of the gear they'd need to bring along. Four flashlights (an extra in case one broke), extra batteries, a camera, two rolls of film, a notebook, pencils, snacks, soda pop, a blanket, a baseball, roller skates, a Frisbee, four or five books they could use to prop open doors (so they didn't get locked inside), and a marker just in case they wanted to leave any mysterious messages inside the desks of any teachers—just to drive them nuts.

"It's going to be a little tricky," he admitted, "because we're not even supposed to *be* there. So step one is we're going to have to sneak in."

They would use their usual alibi. Willie would tell his parents he was sleeping over at James's house. James would tell his parents he was sleeping over at Willie's. Reggie, whose mother worked too late to chaperone any sleepovers, claimed he could do whatever he pleased, and whenever, and so had no use for their lies.

Willie and James were roped into the plan before they had a chance to protest. When James saw that

Reggie had already spent his meager allowance on spare batteries, he got that sick feeling in his gut again. This was really happening. If they were caught for trespassing, could they be expelled? Or even arrested? James didn't know, but his stomach roiled when he thought of disobeying his parents. As exciting as Reggie's plans were, he knew full well that they were part of the hole, not the donut. There was still one hope: it was conceivable that Willie's parents wouldn't permit Willie to sleep over, and James was counting on this to disrupt Reggie's plan. Unfortunately, Willie's parents thought it would be rude to turn down James Wahl's invitation—the Wahls were so respected, after all, and they had such a big, pretty house. In fact, Mrs. Van Allen was sewing shut the left arm of a pair of Willie's pajamas especially for the occasion.

"We'll ditch your pj's on the way," said Reggie impatiently.

Naturally they would have to break the brand-new curfew. For some reason this detail went unspoken among the three friends, though it haunted James. Such concerns did not touch Reggie: he chewed his fingernails, swiped away pink eraser particles, and revised his two-page inventory with a stubby pencil clamped between his knuckles. Frowning, he crossed off "roller skates."

The plan was set for Friday. That way, when Saturday morning arrived, the school would be deserted and they could just crawl out a window, feel the warm summer sun heat their necks, and smile in the knowledge that they had just pulled a fast one—on their parents, their school, the curfew-makers, the hit-and-run driver, every-one.

"If this is our last summer," Reggie reminded them, "I don't want to die without knowing what's behind all those doors."

* * *

Late Friday afternoon, James walked to the Van Allen house to pick up Willie, as always keeping an eye on every truck that rumbled down every side street. When he got there the sky was orange. The deserted tree house towered over him as he climbed the front stairs. James looked at it, saw branches move, heard boards whine.

"That tree house has got to go."

James jumped. Mr. Van Allen was standing on the other side of the screen door, also gazing up at the tree. James felt his heart pound; he had not yet knocked. Mr. Van Allen said nothing and inspected the tree house, perhaps remembering when he'd built it: the coarse feel of the two-by-fours, the temperature of a nail after being struck by a hammer. James glanced at Mr. Van Allen's hands. Thick curly hair swallowed up a giant class ring. The fingernails were notched and dirty. The hand gripped a beer can but had forgotten it—it tipped precariously and James tensed, waiting for liquid to start dribbling.

"How are you, James?" It was said so quietly, James thought he might have imagined it.

"Fine?" James answered.

Mr. Van Allen nodded vaguely, his eyes still searching the tree house lumber.

"You know I love you boys," he whispered.

James held his breath and watched beer gather at the rim of the can.

"You know that. I know you know that." Mr. Van Allen drew a long breath, jutting out his bottom jaw in an apparent attempt to summon strength. "We all make mistakes, James. Every one of us. But that doesn't mean there isn't love."

After a while Mr. Van Allen glanced at James with vacant eyes. An instant later, he walked away. James stood there, his chest thumping, his neck sweating. What was he supposed to do now?

From somewhere inside the house, Mr. Van Allen's voice: "Willie. Friend's here."

Moments later, Mrs. Van Allen let James in, crying, "Well, hello there, stranger!" She came up next to him, taking hold of his shoulder and bouncing her hip against his side, her other arm searching for an opportunity to hug but dangling loose when James made none available. Mrs. Van Allen was a heavy woman with silver hair lopped short. She wore jewelry and makeup, and plenty of both. In years prior, James had thought this decoration made her glamorous, but not anymore. Her cheeks were caked with a substance tan and muddy, and her eyelashes were gloppy with something black and wet. Her mouth was bright red, but the paint went a little past her lips, coloring the surrounding skin so she looked like a clown. In the days since Willie's accident, she was simply *too much*–too bright, too happy, too forceful, too talkative.

"Come in, come in. How nice to see you! How are your mother and father? Will you tell them hello for me? They're such wonderful people, Mr. and Mrs. Wahl."

"They're fine."

"Oh, how wonderful!" she cried, before James had even finished responding. James glanced over at Mr. Van Allen, who now sat at the kitchen table, his back to them, clutching that sweaty beer in that hairy fist. James got the feeling Mrs. Van Allen carried on conversations only to somehow please her husband. It did not seem to be working. A newspaper lay dissected before Willie's father. Certain portions of the print were circled in ink. The only sound was the frustrated ticking of an electric fan. There was a foul smell in the air, like turned meat.

"Hi, James!"

Willie stomped down the hall, an engorged backpack swinging from his good shoulder. Suddenly he lost equilibrium and dipped, his one arm flapping like a stricken bird, before righting himself and laughing. James watched his friend struggle against gravity every day, but it was particularly troubling that something as unthreatening as a backpack could take Willie down.

"William, you have your special pj's?"

"Yes, Momma."

"And you have your toothbrush? You make sure to scrub those braces."

"Yes, Momma."

"And you're sure you don't want to take . . . your bear?"

Everyone knew that Willie's teddy bear was named Softie, but evidently Mrs. Van Allen was trying not to embarrass him. James scowled at her—she never should've mentioned Softie at all. This feeling was followed by frustration at Willie for still having the damn bear in the first place, which is exactly what Reggie had been saying for the last couple years: it was embarrassing, a kid his age.

"No, Momma," Willie said, his ears going red.

"Okay, then, mister. Go kiss your daddy goodbye."

Willie glanced at James, then dutifully scuffed his way across the cluttered living room floor—it didn't *used* to be this cluttered, James observed—and stood next to his father. It was a ritual James had seen a thousand times, one he was glad he didn't have to perform himself: the parting kisses to Mommy and Daddy. Only this time Willie hesitated, just for a second, and James noticed a passing look on Willie's face like he was about to put his lips to something revolting. The fan ticked and Willie's hair swirled.

"Bye, Dad," Willie said, pecking him fast on the cheek. Mr. Van Allen did not stir.

"Willie loves his daddy," said Mrs. Van Allen, grinning down at James. There was a smudge of red lipstick on her teeth as if she had bit into something alive. But when she hugged Willie and kissed him on the ear, the *too much* of Mrs. Van Allen went away and James saw only goodness: her eyes and how tightly they were wrinkled shut, how her swaying arm muscles clenched in the intensity of the embrace, how she ruined her hairdo against Willie without worrying in the slightest.

Willie broke away and called out one more goodbye, and then they were outside. When the two of them were past the tree house, down the drive, and onto the sidewalk, James threw one more peek over his shoulder. Mrs. Van Allen was still standing at the door, grinning and waving, but she was looking the wrong way, bidding goodbye to no one.

* * *

Just before five the three boys stood flat like burglars against a brick wall, behind the bushes. The school doors were not yet locked—the withdrawn bolts were visible even from this distance—and so they continued to wait, and pant, and blink away the sweat. They fixed themselves for an unbearable length of time, motionless in the very spot where they usually ran, silent where they usually shouted, waiting for some signal apparently recognizable to Reggie only.

At last it happened: Reggie drew breath, nodded, extricated his skin from the wall, and moved.

"Act like we're supposed to be here," he said. He lowered his head and moved like a bull. Seeing him so heedless of peril filled James with sudden courage. He slipped through the door first and Willie scampered in behind, thumping his backpack on the doorframe and once more nearly taking a dive. As usual, Reggie came last, and he took a moment to ensure the door made no sound when closing.

The school's primary hallway was not the familiar orchestra of noise to which they were accustomed. Now it was the open throat of a sleeping beast. After not even ten feet, all three boys stopped. For several seconds their footsteps continued to crash off hard surfaces. They stared down the empty distance, unwilling to turn to one another and recognize that frozen look of fright. They held their breath. The silence roared. Finally, they heard faraway thuds.

"Custodians," whispered Reggie.

They moved. When they came to the elbow in the hallway, Reggie held a finger to his lips and moved off to the side. At his signal, all three boys dropped to a knee and removed their shoes, tied the laces together and swung them over their shoulders. When they stood, Willie's knot didn't hold and his shoes hit the floor. James winced. Reggie glowered. Willie grinned in embarrassment, angering Reggie even more, and tried again to tie his laces. It was impossible to do well with one hand, so James leaned over and finished the job.

When they passed the unsecured locker that used to

belong to Greg Johnson, Reggie opened it slowly and together they faced a black emptiness that went on forever.

They reached the milk room, a small chamber near the cafeteria with a warped wooden door that hadn't shut properly in years. Inside was a large unlocked cooler that contained hundreds of identical pink milk cartons. Reggie removed three cartons of 2 percent, passed them out, then set about quietly arranging and stacking dozens of empty milk crates that the boys could hide behind. Then they sat together on the frigid cement, sipping their milk, ears pricked for the stray rumbling of a janitor's mop bucket. The cooler hiccupped and purred. Soon their teeth were chattering.

"It's freezing," whispered Willie.

"Shut up," said Reggie.

They held their breath when keys jangled past the milk room. A few minutes after that, they heard metal clangings. Then more of the same, only farther away. After that, there was no sound beyond the cooler and the careful breathing of the three boys.

"Okay," said Reggie.

They tiptoed out into the hallway. The lights were out. Sunset's glow spread through far-off windows and glared off the tile. They wandered in small circles, blood pounding through their ears.

"HEY!"

James leaped. Willie yelped. They both looked at Reggie, who watched their terrified reactions in delight, his rib cage expanding and collapsing.

James tried it. "HEY, YOU!"

Willie joined in. "HEY, YOU, BUSTER!"

And they continued that way for a while, forcing noise, any kind, into the immeasurable silence.

* * *

It did not last. Soon the boys moved as if through a church, quiet and reverent, afraid to put their hands to anything.

They entered the gymnasium, which tripled as the lunchroom and auditorium. The boys craned their necks to peer into the vast open space. It was dark and deep and swimming with dead lamps and dormant basketball hoops. The boys shifted their eyes away and hurried on. The floorboards complained.

The science lab was locked. They squashed their noses against the glass. Inside, the multiple sinks gleamed in the moonlight. The boys looked toward the case that contained dead beetles, spiders, and butterflies, each stabbed with little colored pins advertising their different parts, but it was too dark to see any bugs. Were they still there? Willie started looking at the ground and instantly the other two boys froze in place.

What if the bugs escaped at night and crawled beneath the door?

"I smell meat, I smell meat," Willie mumbled. The other boys laughed nervously. After a moment, Willie realized what he had said and laughed too.

A few years ago, Willie had discovered how to

memorize schoolwork. All you had to do was make up an unusual sentence that had the same first letters as what you were trying to memorize. For example, in science class—in this very room they were peeking into—Mr. Sharp made them memorize the three different kinds of rocks: igneous, sedimentary, and metamorphic, I-S-M. So Willie invented the phrase "I Smell Meat" to help him remember.

It didn't stop there. In Ms. Janney's social studies class, they had to memorize the first seven presidents. "Where All Jokers Must Make a Jump" stood for Washington, Adams, Jefferson, Madison, Monroe, Adams (John Quincy), and Jackson. Even Reggie still remembered the presidents, and once recited all seven in proper sequence to evade punishment from the principal. James too had benefited from Willie's talent, and felt pride when he saw other kids mouthing the bizarre sentences during tests.

"Kids (Poor Creatures) Often Fight Good Sense" stood for the different levels of the animal world: kingdom, phylum, class, order, family, genus, and species. "Everyone Just Leaves" stood for the three branches of government: executive, judicial, and legislative. The system worked. How else was a kid supposed to remember Precambrian-Paleozoic-Mesozoic-Cenozoic or Dopey-Bashful-Grumpy-Doc-Happy-Sneezy-Sleepy or LCDM, the ascending Roman numerals? He might be shy and small and have bad teeth, a long nose, a neck scar, and only one arm, but nobody could get you through a tough exam like Willie Van Allen.

There was only one problem. His sentences outlasted their usefulness. Willie repeated them so often they became as natural as breathing and as accessible as the alphabet. If you listened, you could hear him murmuring them softly when it was his turn to bat or when Mel Herman wandered too close, smacking gum.

Student artwork lined the hallway leading to the art room. The boys ran their flashlights over each work, exclaiming when they found one of their own. It was fun enough. Eventually one of them noticed that there were several pictures missing. According to alphabetical placement, these spaces had once been claimed by Greg Johnson. Someone had taken his artwork, just like they had taken the contents of his locker, and it was as if he never existed.

"Guys, look at this," said Reggie.

They all gathered around a watercolor painting. It was a swirl of garish color: red, purple, orange, and green, with razor slices of yellow. James and Willie stared for a minute but there was nothing substantial to find within the mess, just haunted outlines and unsettling shapes.

Reggie's flashlight found the signature in the corner, scraped in reluctant pencil: MEL HERMAN.

"Figures," he said.

Mel Herman was a mean kid. He was bigger than his

classmates, and it was speculated that he had once been held back a grade, maybe even two or three. He sat in the back of class, slumped deep down in his desk. Teachers were always telling him to stop looking out the window and pay attention.

Here was the strange thing. All the teachers seemed to like Mel Herman. Maybe this was because he always did well on tests even though he never studied. He could do an entire page of math problems before most kids could finish one or two. You could always tell when Mel finished, because he would snap his pencil in two, sigh loudly, cross his arms, and stare out the window like he'd do almost anything to be set free.

Mel's grimy hair tangled around his ears. He wore thick glasses that were always taped in the corners. He wore the same too-big black shirt day after day. One kid swore Mel used to have a paper route but was fired when he attacked an adult who refused to pay. Another kid said that Mel didn't have any parents and survived at home all alone. Still another claimed Mel had once had an older brother, but that he'd died in a shoot-out—either that or was in the slammer serving fifty-to-life. Maybe that was why the teachers liked Mel Herman so much, maybe they just felt sorry for him.

But James and Reggie didn't feel sorry for him. They hated him. Mel didn't have any friends and didn't deserve any. He always showed up to junkball at the same time they did, like he'd been circling the abandoned vehicles all morning. He was the best hitter around—he hit a home run almost every single time he swung—but still nobody wanted Mel Herman on their team, because if you screwed up, he'd go crazy. He'd yell and scream until his face grew red and his nose dripped snot. Sometimes he'd push you over and rage above you with his hands in fists. Fortunately, instead of trouncing you, he'd usually just invent some bad words and pace around the outfield. In the meantime the game halted, and all the players stood around swatting mosquitoes and wishing they were somewhere else.

It wasn't just the diamond. Without notice, Mel Herman showed up everywhere, all the time, a big black mark that marred any scene he entered. Playgrounds: there he was, shuffling past the jungle gym. The library: he's there, moving among the cold, still stacks. The streets: at the end of every single block, around each corner. Despite the fear and unease he struck in smaller boys everywhere, he moved about the town virtually unnoticed by grown-ups, possibly because he was neither small enough (a lost toddler) nor big enough (a delinquent high schooler) to raise alarm. Grown-ups, of course, were mistaken. This skulking black-clad figure, this mysterious Mel Herman, was a menace, always in motion, always a danger, and always unwelcome.

Mel was also the best artist in school by a mile, although he seemed to hate art class as much as any other. Usually he would paint pictures so overwhelming that they were impossible to appraise beyond their scope and size. There were no rainbows in his artwork, no cats or dogs, no figures holding hands, nothing painted in brush-strokes applied with anything less than murderous force. Mel worked in great, wet, purposeful patterns constructed with a brutal confidence; these formations often paired themselves with details so fine they hurt the eye—even with his artwork, Mel Herman terrorized. Now and then an art teacher would risk offering praise for one of these fanatical images, to which Mel would only stare back, his thick face ripening with disgust.

Other times, mostly in earlier grades, Mel would dash off something awesome—a salivating dinosaur, or a disintegrating vampire, or a guitar flying through the air on Pegasus wings—but then, before showing it to the teacher, he'd tear it to pieces. When the teacher asked him why he hadn't done the assignment, he'd just shrug and say, "The assignment was stupid." Then his eyes would spark behind his dirty glasses and he'd wipe his nose with the back of his sleeve, and all the other kids would busy themselves with their drawings so he didn't catch them watching.

The best Reggie and James could figure, Mel just liked trouble. Saturated in light, isolated from the primitive sixth-grade doodles surrounding it, his painting was as breathtaking as his unannounced arrival at the junkball field. As scary as it was, the painting was truer than anything that anyone at school had ever said, because it came directly from Mel's brain, completely uncontaminated by fears of bad grades, detention, or ridicule. It was as honest as someone spitting in your face.

"Guys."

Reggie's voice was severe. James's and Willie's lights twirled madly across the walls. It was another Mel Herman masterpiece, and this one was huge: four strips of brown paper had been hastily stapled to create a massive, disorderly canvas, and even at this size the activity spilled off all four edges. It looked like a road map drafted by a lunatic. The entire surface was etched with minuscule people, animals, landscapes, and loosely geometric patterns. It was pencil, crayon, paint, and marker, and all mixed together in every possible color. There was even a splotch that just had to be dried ketchup. All the same, James didn't know why Reggie's face was so grim.

"Look," Reggie hissed, jabbing a finger at the picture's bottom left corner. The boys pressed forward. Willie's long nose nearly touched the paint.

James saw a squiggle of lines. Willie's eyes traced the same squiggle. Then Reggie breathed the word "truck" and the suggestion instantly aligned their vision, snared their breath, beat together their hearts, because secretly they were all dying to find exactly what they had found.

It was a tiny drawing of tiny vehicle running over a tiny person. It was a detail so small probably no one had ever noticed it before. Yet there it was.

The boys pointed flashlights into each other's faces. Their skin burned pallid and their eyes became reflecting pennies, their mouths gaping black holes. Willie closed his eyes to block the light and for a second looked like Greg Johnson in his casket, tranquil and colorless.

James tapped Willie's good shoulder with his flashlight until Willie cracked open an eye.

"Do you think . . . ?" James whispered.

"Get that flashlight outta my eyes," Willie said.

"But why would he do it?" said James.

"Why are you trying to blind me?" said Willie.

"Wait a minute, no," James said, shaking his head. "Mel Herman can't drive."

"Why not?" shouted Reggie. His face was grave but his eyes glinted. "He's big enough to drive a truck. Smart enough, too, I bet."

"Maybe his dad drives it," suggested Willie.

The bottom of James's stomach fell away. This was too plausible.

"I thought he didn't have a dad," James said hopefully.

"That's the thing, nobody knows," said Reggie. James could tell he was thrilled to unearth a new reason to hate Mel Herman, and instantly James felt Reggie pushing this reason on him and Willie, pressuring them to accept it. "Nobody knows squat about him. He wears the same clothes every day. He walks to school from who knows where. Hell, he walks *everywhere* and watches *everyone* and knows exactly what everyone is up to. And he shows up for junkball out of *nowhere*?"

The implication was haunting. If Mel Herman followed

kids to the junkyard, might he follow kids away from the junkyard as well? Might he do it in a truck?

Reggie leapt and in a single motion ripped the large painting from the wall. When he folded it into quarters and stuffed it inside his backpack, he moved with the curt motions of one handling something dead.

They did not stay the night. Around midnight, the boys wiggled out a classroom window, and when they walked away from the school they did it swiftly and did not look back.

Parents, Prepare My Cage

They couldn't return home at one in the morning, especially since they were all supposed to be staying at one another's houses. So Reggie, James, and Willie crept through the town toward the park, where they could sleep beneath branches, out of view of any police cruising the streets on the lookout for suspicious curfew breakers or trucks. As they walked, James thought he had never seen the town so static.

They woke up at dawn and stretched, laughing at the strange tattoos the grass left on their faces and forearms. They tried to remember what had happened inside the school, but the memory was as murky as a dream. Only the crackle of Mel Herman's painting inside Reggie's backpack hinted otherwise.

They moved fast, trying to beat the sun across the sky. They passed a woman walking the opposite way down the sidewalk. Two little girls, twins, held on to the woman's hands. When they passed, the girls saw Willie's missing arm and at the exact same time started bawling.

The boys ran.

The Van Allen house was the first stop. The tree house looked small and flimsy in the morning light. Without a word, James and Reggie nodded farewell to Willie and watched as he started up the driveway, his shoes making light patters on the pavement. So delicate, these sounds—but suddenly the front door flew open and Mrs. Van Allen was there, and she shrieked, and then she and Mr. Van Allen came sprinting, she in a fancy nightgown that rippled back to reveal stripes of underwear, he in pajamas that snapped at the air.

They descended upon Willie like they wanted to eat him. Willie took a knee to protect himself from being tackled. Arms wrapped around his back and lips pressed up against his head. "Oh, baby, my little baby!" squealed his mother, while his father gritted his teeth and encircled both of them in his arms, his hands flitting like spiders across their backs. Willie squeezed shut his eyes like it hurt, and James and Reggie believed it—after a moment, they couldn't even see Willie anymore, he had gone missing somewhere inside the clutching arms of his parents. When another minute passed and no reprimands were doled out, not to anyone, the two boys stole away. The Van Allens never acknowledged them.

Willie was whisked inside, stripped, and nudged into the bath by his mother. His parents obviously knew he had not been at James's house last night, but for some reason they did not discuss it. Willie heard his father dial the phone and sigh, "Call off the dogs, the little son of a gun is back." Then he appeared at the bathroom door, but seemed unnerved by his son's nudity and turned his attention to the newspaper and red pen that were clutched in his shaking hands. "All is well," he said, maybe to them, maybe to himself. "Back to work, then, back to work." Mrs. Van Allen smiled but did not respond, and continued washing the grass from her son's hair—bathing in private was something Willie had been forced to relinquish after losing his arm. As she scrubbed, she jabbered mindlessly about things that were of no interest to Willie: heat, humidity, groceries, the upturn of the job market. Willie was tired and had to keep reminding himself to sit up tall so his arm bandages wouldn't get soapy, but upon hearing this last topic he forced himself to contribute. "Did Dad find a job, then?" he asked, feeling very grown-up despite being naked in a tub. His mother laughed through clenched teeth, scrubbing at his neck, soap bubbles swaying from loose strands of her hair like bulbs on a string of Christmas lights. "No, no, no, he hasn't," she whispered. "But jobs aren't everything, are they?"

As Willie's mother re-dressed his stump, Willie tried to block out her voice so he could hear his father moving elsewhere in the house. The only thing he heard was the electric fan. As was often the case these days, Willie started to worry, and that telltale cleft scored the soft skin between his eyebrows. Willie did not know why his dad had lost his job, but suspected it had something to do with the hit-and-run. It seemed like the same day Willie had been struck on the road, his father had been infected with a terminal disease that he was slowly dying of, right here inside this house.

Willie barely remembered getting hit—just that silver truck and how it had floated away. The doctor who sewed up his stump said it was a blessing he didn't re-member more. Mostly, Willie remembered looking up from a hospital gurney, seeing the white ceiling rush by, and then his father's worried, upside-down face. It was then that Willie uttered his first words since the truck hit him: "Dad, how come you forgot me?"

He didn't mean to make his father feel bad. But after he said it, the life had drained from his father's face and it had yet to return. Before his father lost his job, he had sold things—insurance, mostly—and he would sometimes invite Willie into the TV room where he was downing a beer and spinning an old autographed football between two hands, and he would point at the athletes on the screen and make Willie guess how big an insurance policy he would sell that man if he met him.

"A hundred dollars?" Willie would venture.

"A hundred dollars! This is a sportsman we're talking about here! He makes a living getting his butt knocked around the field!"

"A thousand dollars?" At this point, Willie would start to smile. His father's exaggerated distress was comic.

"A thou–? Kid, tell me you're joking. Oh, you're no son of mine, not with a brain that thinks that small, there's just no way. I always thought you looked like somebody else's kid anyway. You are, aren't you? Just level with me."

"I'm not! I'm yours!"

"Prove it. Because I don't believe it. A thousand dollars, unbelievable! Prove to me you're a son of mine, because this, I'm sorry, I cannot swallow."

"I don't know how!" And now Willie would be laughing, louder and louder to match the increasing volume of his father's protestations, and soon his mother would appear at the door, unable to resist the joyful noise.

"I'll prove it," she once said, and winked, and his father had made a growling cat noise, and though Willie didn't get it, they all laughed together, and his father tackled him against the floor and tickled him, asking how much would he pay to insure against *this*? How about *this*?

There had not been such noise in the house for a long time. One day after kissing his dad's cheek before going outdoors, he felt a cold hand grasp his wrist and wrench him back to the kitchen table. Without another arm to brace himself, Willie nearly fell, but his dad kept him aloft by lifting upward on the arm, too hard. His father's loose red eyes aligned themselves with Willie's.

"Listen," he whispered. The beer stink entered Willie's gaping mouth, stole away his breath. His father gripped his wrist even harder, gave it a brisk shake. "This isn't the life for a kid, I know that. You're not all there. Look at you. That isn't right. But what can I do?"

Willie just stared at him, his wrist smarting.

"There's not one thing I can do. If there was information I could give, facts that would actually really truthfully help, don't you think I would volunteer them?"

"Barry." It was his mother, her voice frightened.

"What information—"

"Barry."

The grip on his wrist tightened, unbearable.

"What *facts* could put you back together? Facts don't mean anything. This is something I've learned. One day, Willie, they are going to ask you for the facts." His father nodded slowly, the pale skin of his razor-burned face looking even deader because of the steady, measured movement. "You tell them. The facts, they do not tell the story."

Then his mother was there, releasing his wrist as easily as if she possessed a key, and he was off, away, outside. After the surgery, his mother had changed, too, wide-eyed and open-mouthed and always looking as if she were bracing for impact. Sometimes there would be little moments when Willie's parents seemed normal. Last Saturday Willie and his mother had laughed together at the cartoons and she had grabbed at his socked feet like she used to while he dodged, and just for a second she had looked like the Momma he remembered. And last week Willie's dad had helped him catch a salamander that went zigzagging beneath the back porch. There, under the stairs, with mud on his cheek and chin, Willie's dad had looked just like he used to–funny, laughing, always up for anything. But of late he just slumped through the house in rumpled pajamas, spreading that beery odor–that flat, rotten, bready stink–from his breath, clothes, hair, and skin.

Sometimes Willie forgot that he didn't have a left arm. Before he'd come home from the hospital, the doctor had told Willie that, in time, he would "mourn" his missing arm. Later, Willie had heard that the town mourned Greg Johnson at his funeral. He began to wonder if his left arm was buried somewhere in the same cemetery, and if one day he might stand over his arm's grave, cry a little, read a little bit from the Bible, and then feel a whole lot better because he had finally properly mourned.

Mournful was not how he felt about his missing limb, not now. His father tended to shy away from the daily dressings, glancing at the naked stump like it was a new, unwanted baby that would not stop wailing. But Willie loved the ritual; it was the only thing he still shared with his mother: the daily unwrappings, her tender fingers, the application of cream, her gentle breath on his sensitive skin, the rewrapping—snug but not too. What else was there? The chores she formerly assigned were too difficult to execute with one arm, and though he gamely tried washing dishes, folding clothes, and clipping coupons, what should have taken minutes lasted hours. She had little use for him indoors, that was clear, but she also did not want him running around outside. Locks on doors were used with frequency, and those doors that did not have locks were given them. Willie assumed his parents feared that the hit-and-run driver would return to finish him off, even though they never dared speak such fears aloud. Even after Greg Johnson had been killed and both Van Allen parents had returned home from the town meeting, they turned away in distaste when Willie had asked too many questions.

So he did not spend much time missing his arm. He spent much more time trying to keep his room clean (which took longer without a left arm), make his bed (that took longer, too), smile a whole lot, and in general be a very good boy, which he hoped might please his parents and rouse them from their sleepwalking. He carried Softie around whenever he could. He wasn't much interested in the teddy bear anymore, but his mom seemed to delight in seeing him with it, so he kept it, despite the mean things Reggie said. He tried to avoid Mel Herman, not because he hated him like everyone else, but because he feared his mother's strange, heartbroken reaction whenever he came home with gum in his hair. It was exhausting, all the things he did each day to keep his parents as happy as possible. Was it normal for a kid to worry that his mother and father would burst into tears at any moment? Wasn't it supposed to be the other way around?

Willie wasn't sure. So he kept smiling and laughing and being good, while privately wondering why his parents were the ones who acted like they had lost something.

* * *

"Willie's mom called here at the crack of dawn to check up on him," James's mother said as she set down his milk and cereal. James had arrived just as his mother was finishing up her own breakfast of grapefruit, toast, marmalade, and tea. Not having had time to reapply makeup after eating, the scar on her upper lip was more visible than usual. James forced himself not to look at it. It upset his mother greatly, this scar; she masked it with more vigor and effort than Willie ever put into trying to hide his stump: cosmetics, lipstick, a raised glass of wine, a knuckle placed to make it look like she was thinking. How a tiny sliver of flesh could be so shameful was unfathomable to James, but it was a flaw, and that was something his mother was not skilled at handling.

Mr. Wahl stood at the other end of the table, having been dragged in there by his wife to be present for this interrogation. But he had brought with him his work, those thousands of tiny numbers, and he stood above his papers with both hands planted flat. There was paper and pens and a calculator, none of which were good signs.

James opened the cereal but could not imagine eating. He had disobeyed his parents and they had caught him. His stomach churned and shook, and he needed to use the toilet. But he was not ready to give in, not quite yet.

"I was rather surprised to receive the call," continued his mother, "because of course I thought you two were over at Willie's."

"Keep your eye on the donut," his father said flatly, his eyes never leaving the numbers. He fished a pen from his ink-stained shirt pocket. "You screw up now, it'll set you on the wrong path for high school, and that's the launch pad for college. That's all it is, kid, nothing more."

James sighed, taking care to make it sound authentic. "I know."

His mother arched an eyebrow as he busied himself with arranging the correct proportion of milk to cereal– without Louise around, it was easy to pour too much of both. His father continued computing his lists of numbers; James could see the mental mathematics tug at his eyes. This was nearly every weekend in the Wahl house: his father consumed with his work and his mother struggling to fill the domestic void left by Louise, who was off on weekends. James remembered when he was very little watching his mother try to hang laundry on a windy day. It was a chore she had not been required to do as a youth, and as a young wife it was something at which she had no facility. James remembered the brisk wind and how the snapping sheets fought his mother's grasping hands, spinning and thickening until she stood defeated before the twisted, anguished cords. Shortly thereafter they hired Louise, a trained nurse who just happened to be an excellent cook and housekeeper.

Weekends also meant no talking about the hit-and-run driver, Louise's favorite topic. The ex-nurse was chatty by nature and happily oblivious to other people's discomfort, and so during the week they often discussed over dinner the ongoing hunt for the killer. With Louise gone, it was verboten. James had the notion that his parents found the subject too vulgar for their table. Unless, of course, they were complaining about how much everyone else in town talked about it–that was fair game. James tried to understand. He knew that neither of his folks had living parents of their own; he had also formed the impression that before he was born there had been other babies who had died while still inside his mother. He was all they had, James knew it. There was no one else left to make them proud.

"So you feel like telling me where you were?" his mother asked.

James sighed again. He and Reggie had come up with an excuse on the way home and now was the time to try it. "Willie and me–"

"Willie and I," his mother corrected.

"Willie and I ended up staying at Reggie's," he said, doing his best to appear sincere. His mother raised her eyebrow higher. "Don't worry," he added, "we were inside before curfew."

James glanced at his father and was surprised to see that his father's eyes had stopped moving. In fact, his entire face and body had gone rigid. This was alarming—although his dad was deadly serious about focusing on the donut, he also took pleasure in James's occasional misbehavior, often comparing it with his own wild escapades, most of them set in college, before hastily changing his tone and adding an obligatory "mind your mother." Normally his father would have shrugged off an offense like last night's curfew-breaking, but this time something was different. Something about the mention of Reggie's house had his father on edge.

James's mother scrutinized her son's face. He stared down at his cereal and lodged some more in his mouth, his stomach squirming.

"You can call Reggie's mom and ask her," he said between crunches. This was his secret weapon: he knew his mother hated calling Reggie's mom. Not only did James's mother think Reggie Fielder was a bad influence, but she also seemed to have a low opinion of his mother. Once James had overheard her saying that "every guy in town" knew Kay Fielder. James knew the reason was something more than the fact that she worked at a restaurant. He had seen plenty of boyfriends come and go from Ms. Fielder's life, including two significant enough to compel her to move both herself and Reggie into the men's houses before moving back out a few months later.

James was not sure his gamble would pay off. His mother looked suspicious. Maybe it was because it was the weekend–his mother grew bolder in the absence of Louise–but all at once James could quite clearly envision his mom calling up Ms. Fielder, not caring for one second that she was probably waking her up. He felt a familiar panic that the road map of his life, so carefully drafted by his parents, was in jeopardy. He thought mournfully of his mother's scrapbook. While his early years were thick with baby announcements, baptism notifications, school chorus programs, and tennis camp certificates, around age ten he appeared to have stagnated. Over the past couple of years only a handful of items had made the pages, leaving far too many blank for high school and college, more than he could ever fill. James felt that this was his fault–he was blowing it, he was losing traction, everything was falling down the damn hole.

He had to stop his mother from calling, and so he did something mean. He looked his mother in the eye, waited until he had her full attention, and then flicked his gaze at her scar. Immediately she covered her mouth with a hand and turned away, making a flat noise kind of like laughter, but not quite. It was the same noise she made when his father made a cruel comment about her looks, or an innocent comment that she took the wrong way. James didn't know how he felt being allied with his father in this fashion. All boys wanted to be grown up, he thought, but did it mean having to feel like this?

"No, I won't call her," his mother said. Her face looked caught, flustered, and she added as if to excuse herself, "She works late."

She took a pinch of James's shoulder.

"But you know how I feel about you staying there," she said.

"Yes, Mom," James said.

"It's just not a good environment for children."

"Yes, Mom," James said.

"I know you don't understand now, but there's certain things you don't need to be exposed to—"

"*Goddammit.*" It was his father's voice, loud and unexpected. "You mind your mother or I swear to you there will be grief."

James's mother's hand slid from his shoulder.

"And why are you covering up your face?" he demanded of his wife. "Why do you always do that? Am I that terrible?"

There was a sound like rubber, his mother's foot pivoting on the waxed floor. Then she was gone, moving swiftly through the house. Faraway stairs thumped, banisters creaked. James crunched his cereal for a moment, staring into the milky glow of his spoon. No one was calling anyone, he was safe, but he felt less secure than ever. He chanced a peek at his father.

His father was staring right at him. His hands were still positioned on either side of the numbers. His body had not moved an inch.

"You were at Reggie's house last night," he said. His voice was soft but direct.

James moved his jaw around the cereal. "Yes."

"Reggie Fielder's house," his father said.

The cereal crackled inside James's mouth.

"Last night," his father said.

His father knew he was lying. James sat there with half-chewed cereal bloating on top of his tongue, trying to figure out where his plan had gone wrong and waiting for the trouble to start.

But his father said nothing. Instead, he lowered his head back at his numbers. After a moment he snatched up his pen and put it to paper. Ink moving too fast: it was the sound of a rattlesnake's approach.

When James dared chew again, the noise was deafening.

* * *

When Reggie got home, his mother was on her back on the sofa, her small white feet hanging over the end. A pillow rested on top of her face. She still wore her waitress uniform; Reggie saw the multicolored splatters of other people's food. A cigarette was dying on a dinner plate on the floor.

"Reg?" Her voice was muffled. This was how she

liked to sleep. Sometimes Reggie went for days without seeing her face.

"What."

She yawned and weaseled her body deeper into the cushions.

"There's chicken-fried steak in the fridge."

Reggie looked longingly at the TV and the stereo. He wouldn't be allowed to turn on either until his mom went back to work at eleven, a whole lifetime away. He tossed his backpack onto the grubby carpet—he barely even noticed the rustle of Mel Herman's painting inside—and sat in the cushionless rocking chair. With his toe he shoved aside the clay ashtray he had made his mother in art class several years ago, and put his feet up on the busted heater that currently served as their coffee table. He stared at his mother's body.

"I was at James's house last night, in case you were wondering."

She didn't respond. Smoke hung in the air above her head like an empty comic book balloon.

"Actually, I was at Willie's," he said. He waited to see if this change in story would get a reaction.

Her toes curled, then straightened.

"Poor kid," she mumbled through the pillow. Reggie didn't know if she was referring to him or Willie. Over the past few years, as she had taken more shifts and responsibility at work, her interest in Reggie's life had seemed to drift away. She resumed a momentary interest following Willie's accident, and for a few weeks had talked about the hit-and-run driver incessantly, badgering Reggie with questions that he was only too happy to try to answer. Reggie even brought Willie by at the beginning of the summer so his mom could gasp and shriek and ask him an almost unending series of inappropriate questions. "What was it like waking up without an arm?" "Do you feel sometimes like it's still there?" "How much does an arm weigh? I mean, how much weight did you lose after it came off?"

It was embarrassing for Reggie, but Willie didn't seem to mind. Then she was off to work, and had barely mentioned the hit-and-run driver since, though this could be because she heard it nonstop from diners at the restaurant. She might just be sick of it.

Reggie stood up and moved to her side. He watched his mother's chest rise and fall, rise and fall. She was smaller than almost any mother Reggie had ever seen, and younger, too. Reggie was born when his mother was only seventeen, which meant she wasn't yet thirty. Reggie supposed she was pretty as moms go, which explained the attraction for James and Willie, but he wished she would eat more. She got skinnier and skinnier, which made no sense—she worked at a restaurant! Reggie figured if he worked there he'd be eating burgers and fries and chocolate malts all day long.

Beneath the pillow, he could see the blond waves of her hair. She spent a lot of time in the mirror messing with it. She'd put junk in it and tie it up above her head.

Then she'd let it back down and toss it around her shoulders. Her hair was always flickering about, probably because she had a bouncy step and wore shoes with remarkable heels. When Reggie was younger and she couldn't find a babysitter, she'd bring him to the restaurant and plunk him down in a corner booth with a stack of coloring books. Reggie, though, would spend most of the evening watching her as she bounced around the restaurant with her blond locks swinging. Reggie couldn't believe how happy she looked, how widely she smiled at complete strangers, how loudly she laughed when they made jokes. After a while, Reggie started laughing, too. But in the car after work, there was no laughter. She sat in the driver's seat, counting change.

"I must be an awful waitress," she muttered.

"I think you're really good," Reggie ventured.

"What do you know about waitressing?" she snapped, stuffing the money into her purse. It had been a great effort for her, getting a job at one of the nicer restaurants in town. Reggie knew she worked her ass off trying to get better shifts. She spent spare time studying library books about wine. She even tried to convince her boss to class up the joint by retiring those tacky uniforms. But it seemed to Reggie that every month there was a setback—some boss dangling the position of assistant manager only to give it to someone else, some shift supervisor patting her on the butt, that hostess position they would not give to her no matter how badly she begged.

In the V-neck of the uniform, Reggie could see her chest bones. Resting on her sternum was a golden heart-shaped locket. It was green in spots. One of her hands rested alongside the locket and the fingernails were painted pink, but the polish was chipped. She wore three rings but none of them was a wedding band. She had left Reggie's father before Reggie was old enough to remember. Now he knew only that his father was in prison and that he was never to speak of him to anyone, least of all her boyfriends, whom she went through at a relatively set pace—about one per year. She brought these men home with increasing infrequency, which Reggie appreciated even while it made him nervous: he no longer knew how serious she was getting with any of them. Now his fear was that at any moment she would announce that they were once again moving all their junk into some strange man's house. Reggie promised himself that the next time she made such an unfair demand, he would refuse. It was that simple. He could live on his own if necessary. He could sleep in the tree house. James and Willie would bring him food. It could work.

Both of his best friends still inquired about his mom, like you would ask after an old friend who moved away. His mother had been something of a celebrity to James and Willie ever since they were little because she had treated them like equals instead of brats. She asked them about their classmates and their teachers, and didn't hesitate to call either group Miserable Bastards or Giant

Bitches. She would let them look on as she arranged her hair, as she picked out her makeup; she'd ask them what color she should go with before squatting with them on the carpet and painting her toenails. She told James and Reggie to call her Kay, and every time they called her Ms. Fielder she crossed her eyes and pretended to gag.

Reggie hated it. He hated watching his mother, still wet from the shower and wrapped in bath towels, as she adorned herself in the clothes and hair of a movie star. It simply was not what moms were supposed to do. The whole thing was humiliating for him, but it was the "Kay" that upset him the most. She was a mother, she was "Mom," and she was all Reggie had, and by calling her Kay, James and Willie stole even that away from him. If she really was Kay, then Mom must be dead and gone. James and Willie did not get it—they even nicknamed her Call-Me-Kay, which Kay herself found adorable—and so Reggie had no other option but to keep his friends away from the house as much as possible. James's place, Willie's tree house, the junkyard: all of these were better options, because Call-Me-Kay would not be there.

Now it did not matter, because she was hardly ever home. All at once Reggie didn't like seeing that pillow over his mother's face. It reminded him of a casket lid. Nervously, he reached down and slowly lifted it away.

There she was, Mom, her painted eyes closed, her pink lips parted, a bead of drool hanging at the corner of her mouth. Her eyelashes fluttered, then her green eyes squinted open, and she looked at Reggie like she had never seen him before.

After a moment she spoke in a hoarse voice. "What's the matter?"

Reggie shrugged.

"I could only see your hair."

She frowned, closed her eyes again, and turned to nuzzle the back of the sofa.

"Maybe I oughta cut it off," she mumbled.

Reggie pictured her standing in front of the bathroom mirror, sawing off all that pretty hair with a pair of rusty scissors, and suddenly his legs felt trembly and liquid. He wanted to lie down next to his mother, right now. He didn't even care if he got other people's food all over him.

"Lemme sleep, Reg," she said. Her hand reached out and clawed the air.

After a moment, Reggie held out the pillow so her hand could snatch it. She pressed the pillow back down over her face. Moments later Kay was snoring.

Desperate Boys Get Destroyed—Hated, Stubborn, Stupid

*M*ost rumors about Mel Herman are not true. He did not put a kindergarten kid into traction. He did not light a cow on fire so he could watch the thing thrash about the field before falling over in a smoldering pile. He did not slash the wheels of the gym teacher's car. He did not eat a live mouse, bones and all. He did not refuse an offer to join the training camp of a professional baseball team.

But one rumor is true. He did, once upon a time, have a paper route. It is three years ago: each morning, a white van deposits a thick slab of bound newsprint on Mel Herman's front lawn, and he wakes up before dawn to roll and rubber-band the newspapers—roll, *snap,* roll, *snap*—before piling them with ink-stained fingers into a huge sack that he balances atop his shoulders before hitting the pavement.

The paper route ends just over a year after it began, when Mel slings a rolled-up newspaper with such force that it punches a neat hole in someone's front window. Intrigued by this achievement, and fascinated by the near-perfect roundness of the wound in the glass, he tries it again a couple houses down. This time an entire living room window explodes, leaving behind a mesmerizing pattern of shards clinging to the window frame—conjoined triangles like mountain ranges, swooping curves like ocean waves, pointy spindles like rows of sharks' teeth. Like magic, the window becomes something he could stare at all day, though of course he can't—here comes the patter of slippered feet and a woman's screech, and so Mel beats hell out of there, knowing it is the last time he'll toss newspapers, which is a real shame now that some good finally came of it.

That night, after being summoned to the newspaper office and fired, Mel goes home, closes his bedroom door, removes his battered lunch box of paint and brushes, and paints his memory of the two destroyed windows. He finds that, once shattered, the window can be reconstructed in a million different ways, and that the points of broken window do exactly that, they *point,* to other destinations of glassy perfection and smashed ruin. This connecting-the-dots is art to Mel Herman, though he does not call it art. He just does it, quickly and for the record, as another kid might jot a diary entry.

After that final day of the paper route, Mel Herman paints what he sees, and he sees when he walks, so it's simple—he just never stops walking. These days he paints so forcefully that sometimes the brush splits to daggers in his hand. It used to be different. He used to draw what other kids drew: fantasy things, normal things, things you didn't need to walk the town to appreciate. Long before leaving for the big city in the middle of the night a few years ago, Mel's brother, five years older than Mel, used to emerge from his private, padlocked room of smoke and smells and music, and make fun of Mel's paintings. You sissy, you queer, you girl. But Mel kept on, and soon his brother started shrugging from behind his cigarettes and tossing record albums on Mel's bed. "Draw something like that," his brother said. "I'm gonna need some album art pretty soon." Mel complied, and when he heard his brother's guitar making noises from behind that padlocked door, Mel turned that noise into paint.

Then his brother dropped out of high school and skipped town. Mel kept painting; he'd come back, Mel was sure of it. And a few weeks later, his brother did return, his face ash, his arms skinny, his fingers twitching, his busted jack-o'-lantern grin looser and hungrier than ever. Through a mouthful of nicotine and beer suds Mel's brother reported that his band was practicing all the time in the city, they were loud and incredible, and they'd need some album art real soon, Mel, so keep it up, man, keep it up. His brother left again, and Mel kept it up.

When his brother next returned it was nearly a year later, and he was all pelvis and vertebrae and jawbone, with skin as dry and scratchy as that brown paper they made Mel paint on at school. His brother smelled rancid and his teeth were gray, and the long hair that was his pride was patchy and clung together in slippery clumps. Several of his brother's fingertips were burned so badly there were black holes in the skin. Mel mentioned it—he was worried it would impede guitar playing. "Matches" was all that his brother said, while hacking and spitting snot and rubbing warmth back into his shaking elbows. There was less talk about the band this time, more talk about how bad he needed money. Their father, as usual, would give him nothing—especially if Mel's brother was going to use the cash to ruin himself with odious habits. After a late-night shouting encounter on this topic, Mel's brother escaped again beneath the stars, and he left without taking any of the dozens of paintings Mel had made for his band.

So he stopped painting album covers and started painting the world. Those two busted windows flash in his memory. Mel is impatient for another such opportunity to present itself, so he begins carrying a fist-sized rock in his shirt pocket, and with every step the rock swings and beats against his heart, *bump, bump, bump, bump,* until by the end of the day the skin there is tender and blue, and until, after a while, the bruise is replaced with a patch of skin thicker and harder. This weapon against his heart strengthens him with every step. His heart is stone.

One day he throws the rock to scare off a frothing dog with crossed eyes that slinks out from the abandoned train depot. Mel is older now and a rock seems kind of stupid anyway, so he replaces it with something better: the padlock still hanging loose from his brother's bedroom door. Mel finds that his hand curls nicely around the cold metal, and that it feels good how powerfully his middle finger grips the upper loop. Tucked into his clenched palm, it turns Mel's fist to metal. Hidden back inside his shirt, Mel's heart turns to metal, too; the new weapon beats ruthlessly against him as he takes each one of the thousands of steps that moves him around the town: *thunk, thunk, thunk, thunk.* To hide it he finds an old black shirt of his brother's and wears it over the top of his clothes nearly every day.

Then it is Christmas Eve and Mel is passing through the town square with his chin tucked low inside the black shirt, and he comes upon a familiar plaster scene: Mary, Joseph, angels, shepherds, a baby. He chooses one of the wise men. He reaches below his brother's shirt and removes his heart. In his hand the padlock is so icy cold that it feels ten times heavier, and before this powerful sensation of heaviness leaves him, Mel punches and punches, losing the padlock in the madness, and there is new destruction, plenty of it, if only he can remember all of it for later: tiny white facial features, golden bits of costuming, two hands still locked in prayer formation. That night he paints, but the dismembered wise man looks too much like his brother. Mel feels stupid and lonely and, after a while, agitated. He finds he misses that familiar weight against his chest, so he rummages through his brother's room until he finds a new object, this one even larger and more dangerous. He puts it beneath the black shirt next to his heart.

Now it's summer—the bloody summer of Greg Johnson and Willie Van Allen—and Mel Herman walks, and looks, and listens. He still leaves home each day at sunrise, and tiptoes out so as not to wake his father—he can hardly bear the thought of seeing the old man in the full light of day—and returns shortly before dark, when his father's phlegmy voice shouts for him to come closer. Until then Mel will not think of it; he shuts it away in the back of his mind. Though he no longer lugs a sack of newspapers, Mel still keeps to his old route, every day. It is a hot summer and his nose is sweaty; he pushes his taped glasses upward and walks faster.

He is glad it is summer. Teachers sicken him, especially the new art teacher, Mr. Camper, with his beard, long hair, and rolled-up flannel shirt sleeves, and his insistence that his students call him by his first name— "Bud"—not to mention the way he has of praising Mel's work and then looking at him as if waiting on Mel's response, a response that Mel goes out of his way to withhold. Teachers, including Mr. Camper—"Bud"—have always claimed to like Mel's stuff, but they never really look at it for more than a few brief moments. *It's all in there,* Mel wants to scream at them, as they blabber about his talent and hang his oversize paintings in the school hallway along with all the other worthless junk. *If you would just look, you'll see everything—you, me, this town, my missing brother, my furious father, and all the terrible things that happen that no one ever wants to see.* These thoughts shoot through his brain. But when he opens his mouth, only foul words come out, and then even Mr. "Bud" Camper looks at him in exasperation and disappointment.

Kids are even worse. Mel detests them. Often he overlooks his hatred and plays junkball with them and has fun, even convincing them to try big-league plays like the sacrifice fly and the hit-and-run, until he recognizes that animal fear in their eyes. In a way, Mel is glad the other kids are afraid. As long as they are afraid they will not come close enough to learn his secrets, like the new weapon hanging hard across his chest, or how his brother shriveled to a living corpse before vanishing into the city, or the greatest secret of all: the truth about his father.

If Mel needs to frighten them, or punch them, all right, fine, good.

So he spends most of his time with grown-ups. Each summer Mel works odd jobs for some of the same people who used to be on his paper route; this is partly why Mel always seems to be everywhere, roving, absorbing, recording everything for translation into paint. At first he refused to spend all of his time laboring, but his father does not work and starves for money like animals starve for food, and so Mel takes on the jobs, scraping scum from an above-ground pool, knocking dried mud from trucks, pushing a lawn mower around some guy's colossal backyard. Initially Mel is concerned about what these people say—about him ("You're far too big for sixth grade"), about his brother ("He seemed to me like a decent kid before he got mixed up in a bad scene"), sometimes even about his father.

Mel relaxes when he realizes that few grown-ups seem to notice him. They talk around him like he's not there. After a while, he observes a curious thing. In the mornings, grown-ups love their town and can hardly believe their dumb luck for having landed here. Then the morning bleeds into day and as the temperature rises their contentment splits and frazzles, and by the second cup of coffee it is not a nice town, not at all, it is a dangerous place where no one in their right mind would want to live. These grown-ups look right through Mel Herman and size up one another—the cement truck driver looks at the parking meter attendant, the parking meter attendant looks at the pharmacist's assistant, and so on—and then they all smile and nod hello, but deep down feel suspicion and resentment. *You cannot trust these people,* their looks say to Mel. *Not these days you can't.* Mel keeps his mouth shut, accepts his meager money, and shuffles away with a sneer curling his lips, because for once the grown-ups are right. He continues down the road, the lethal heaviness beneath his brother's black shirt beating into his heart, *bam, bam, bam, bam.*

What the grown-ups are afraid of is what happened to Greg Johnson. Mel Herman knows a thing or two about Greg Johnson. He knows that the kids of the town hardly think about Greg at all anymore; when Mel cuts through the playground he never hears Greg's name, not ever. But the grown-ups can talk of little else, and so the name churns above the kids like irksome mosquitoes: Greg Johnson, Greg Johnson, Greg Johnson.

Mel works for a woman named Miss Bosch. She is old and seems even older. She lies motionless beneath damp sheets all day in front of a chugging metal fan. Whorls of hair cling wet to her face. Mel goes once a day to check on her. That's it—to check and see if she is okay. Mel guesses his real job is to make sure Miss Bosch hasn't died. Occasionally she asks for something, a tiny wafer of food or another cup of water, and when the task is completed she is as likely to frown at him as to smile. She talks sometimes, too, and if she's feeling well enough, she asks questions. She asks if they've found the hit-and-run killer. Mel says no. She asks if it's true that grown-ups have taken it upon themselves to patrol their neighborhoods night and day, and meet together weekly to discuss any suspect strangers. Mel says yes, he has seen it. She sighs resentfully and gives him a look, and asks if he thinks these patrols are a good use of time.

Mel doesn't know, so he sneaks up to one of these gatherings of grown-ups. He finds them at a house with a back porch and fenced-in yard, with plenty of space for lawn chairs and coolers and children. The grown-ups sit together mostly in silence, while the kids dodge around the lawn, whooping and grasping at fireflies and tumbling and skinning extremities. Mel is so close to the grown-ups he can smell the liquor and barbeque sauce on their words, but he is not afraid, because he has that weight on his chest and will use it if necessary.

The grown-ups are unhappy with the police, who have no leads in finding the killer. They talk of the Van Allens, only briefly, and only in the lowest of tones. The Van Allens, they say, are not doing well, not at all. But their voices brighten when they speak about the Johnsons, who despite their woeful loss are setting a wonderful example with their nightly patrols up and down neighborhood streets. The grown-ups claim they will invite the Johnsons over sometime. Not now, it's too soon. But sometime, the grown-ups are sure of it.

Mel tells all this to Miss Bosch. He describes how easy it is to spot one of these grown-ups on patrol, because of how absurdly slow they always drive, their bug-eyed, oscillating faces, and the languid, glacial crunch of their tires inching across gravel. Miss Bosch looks a little mean when she laughs and Mel Herman likes that.

Mel also hears things from the other grown-ups who employ him. Mel is at their house ripping up the dining room linoleum when Mr. and Mrs. Huron return from a town meeting about the curfew, angrier than when they left. Mrs. Huron stomps upstairs, Mr. Huron heads out back, and the children are left alone with the only thing they care about anyway, their mountain of clattering plastic.

Mel is there soaking up water in her flooded kitchen when Ms. Daisy prepares to take her turn on neighborhood patrol, screwing on a large, flowered hat, unrolling long smooth gloves, and patting herself down before picking up her purse and car keys. When she catches herself in the mirror, Mel sees what Ms. Daisy sees: the ridiculous and elaborate costume of someone totally unequipped to catch a killer.

Mel is there on a ladder, brushing cobwebs from the gutters, when through the open window he hears Mr. Coleman shake his neighborhood patrol schedule and shout into the phone, "Well, is it your turn, Dave? Or is it mine?" Weeks later, after one grown-up reportedly falls asleep on patrol and topples a mailbox, Mel sees Mr. Coleman rip his schedule from the bulletin board and crinkle it into the phone receiver. "I'm not going to have some idiot running over my kid!"

They are all part of Mel's town and are duly incorporated into large paintings made on that scratchy brown paper Mr. "Bud" Camper, for some reason, keeps giving to Mel for free. Some of these paintings hang in school hallways. Most of them are rolled up and stuffed inside Mel's closet. But all of them are evidence. Look closely. Mr. and Mrs. Huron are rust-colored piping shooting off in opposite directions near the center of the town. Ms. Daisy is a bronze star made from shimmering sparkles, then snuffed with charcoal. Mr. Coleman is an angry red spiral that spins inward until he swallows his own burning tail. Of course Miss Bosch is there, too, a yellow skeletal shape with limbs so long they connect to and become every road, street, and alley, granting her miraculous escape despite the fact that she does not leave the bed.

Everything else can be found on these maps, too. Kids he knows. Places he's been. Things he's seen. Fights. Parties. His father. Blood spots on the pavement. As he has almost told "Bud"—and *would* tell him if he didn't so strongly distrust the bearded, long-haired, sleeve-rolled art teacher—the facts are all there for the seeing, if only someone bothered to look.

Last Chances Don't Matter

James and Willie were not much interested in high schoolers, except one. His name was Tom, and for months it had been said that Tom had in his possession a monster. Details were sketchy and sources unreliable, but it was generally agreed that the monster was dead. What remained unclear was what kind of monster it was, and where Tom had found it. Several kids who had older siblings claimed to have seen pictures (grainy, out-of-focus, dark), and one kid claimed to have a sister who touched it and woke up the next day with a rash.

Reggie too was interested in Tom, though in a different

way than James and Willie. Reggie was fascinated with all teenagers and spoke to them whenever he could, sometimes abandoning his friends when he saw a group of older kids across the street. More than one junkball game had been disrupted when a group of teens came by with burning cigarettes and bottled beverages, causing Reggie to lodge his glove in his armpit and go dashing off to greet them.

Reggie used the Monster only as an excuse to muse aloud about the teenagers, what they were doing, the kinds of things they said, banal descriptions of their hair and skin and clothes. Meanwhile, the other kids, including James and Willie, would try to steer the conversation back to where it belonged. "I heard that it's a baby monster," said James. Willie added, "What phylum or species does it belong to, do you think?"

As spring yielded to summer, and the frenzied classrooms gave way to the quiet immensity of the town, the Monster was forgotten. But then came the hit-and-runs. The curfew-shortened days now had to be plotted carefully and spent judiciously, and the Monster was something concrete one could plan to see, go to see, then see.

It was James who first proclaimed, "Let's go see the Monster!" It was after they had stayed overnight at the school and finished off several other escapades, and Reggie was starting to look bored and impatient. This was a dangerous state of mind for Reggie to be in, and it made James nervous. He could see it in the angry line of Reggie's lips, his sudden, short outbursts, the way he hurled rocks at things he shouldn't. There was abuse coming, James could feel it, and so he suggested seeing the Monster merely as something to occupy Reggie's mind. Once spoken, Reggie pounced on the idea and suggested tomorrow as being as good of a day as any, then turned to Willie for confirmation. James knew this trick. Willie would be flattered that he was consulted first and would agree to anything Reggie said. On cue Willie grinned and nodded and went on braiding dandelion stems. "See the Monster, see the Monster," he sang to himself, as if it were nothing more than words.

It was increasingly difficult for Willie to get permission to leave the house these days—once or twice a week there were rumors of a truck gunning its engine outside the schoolyard or across from the park—but the boys managed by promising to bring Willie back before lunch. The next day the three boys set off in the morning, taking turns lugging the backpack full of sandwiches they had assembled, poorly, in James's kitchen without any help from Louise. Reggie ate his sandwich before they were even two blocks from home and ended up sputtering out much of it when Willie flung an acorn at a squirrel, lost his balance, and fell. Willie got up, patted himself off with his one hand, grinned self-consciously, and asked for his sandwich, too. James kneeled down to fish it from the backpack and glanced up to catch Willie touching his stump and wincing.

At Buchanan Street they stopped to buy orange sodas and when they stepped back outside they threw their hands over their eyes. The summer, unbelievably, was hotter.

Tom lived at the end of a long dirt pathway that winded for so long the boys lost sight of it among the weeds. By the time the old farmhouse leapt into view their one wish was to hurry and rinse themselves in its cool shadow. Only when they were leaning beneath a kitchen window, sweat cooling on their legs and broken spiderwebs tickling their necks, did they see everyone standing alongside the old barn. There were teenagers, several loose groups of them, sitting on car hoods, checking their reflections in chrome, drumming their feet in time with the radio, kneeling to touch the matted fur on the back of a farm cat, slinging rocks up at the silo and dodging them as they returned. Beyond these groupings was still another one: three smokers, standing in a half-circle, shoulder to shoulder, staring down at something.

James pushed himself through a web of gnats and heard the other two boys follow.

Their arrival was greeted with indifference. They were ignored, given less respect than the cats. James kept walking, his eyes sweeping across the trail of cigarette butts. A high school–aged boy stepped away from the group and met them shortly before they reached the thing on the ground. He was short and stocky with black hair that grew like moss, almost joining his eyebrows and spilling over onto his cheekbones. There was a pink patch of pimples on his chin. His eyes, while soft, were slightly crossed and slid from the sky to the boys to the dirt and back up again. This was Tom.

"A dollar," he said, but instead of holding out a hand he stuffed both fists into his pockets.

James looked at him for a moment, then turned to Reggie, then Willie. A what? A dollar? What could he possibly mean?

"Aw, come on," said Tom, glancing back at the three smoking teenagers who still stood swaying. Tom sighed and raced his mismatched eyes over the boys before retreating them back to the dirt. "I been giving freebies all day. I ain't doing this for my health."

James fought to make sense of it. How could something as unique as the Monster exist in the same universe as dollars and cents? "We bought orange sodas" was all he could think of to say.

This appeared to make sense to Tom. He grimaced and ran a hand over his neck, then nodded as if he had expected this, as if he had heard it a million times before.

"Well get over there and see it," Tom said. "But I ain't doing this for my health. A guy's gotta make some cash, right? How about next time you pay double? I'm not asking for a lot, but it's summer." Understanding dawned in James. Maybe it cost money to be a part of this world, to drive a car, wear these kinds of clothes, associate with girls. Maybe there were fees connected to growing up that he had yet to consider. He had a sudden urge to discuss it with Reggie, for it seemed possible that Reggie knew of these fees and had begun payment.

But then they were looking down at the Monster, the three of them, and for a while they were silent. The teenagers beside them drifted away after a time but the boys did not notice. They looked, blinked, looked again, and tried to understand what they were seeing.

Willie was the first to speak. "Where did it come from?"

Tom dragged himself closer, glancing at the Monster almost disdainfully. He snorted and spit and stared off into a patchy field where several skinny horses stood motionless. When Tom spoke, it was quick, like something memorized.

"My grandpoppa died last winter and he used to own this land, all of it, far as you can see. Raised horses mainly. When he died we got to go through his things and he had stuff in his attic, crazy stuff, stuff you would probably pay *ten* dollars to see." Tom glanced at them and added ominously, "He was in the *war*."

Tom continued. "This was up there in a big trunk. I can't say for sure what it is or where he got it, but my grandpoppa, he went all over the world, saw all kinds of stuff, so there's really no telling. My guess is that this is from Africa. Or Asia. I guess it don't really matter."

There was a weird buzzing from the teenagers and James turned to look at them—he had forgotten they were there. The young men exchanged looks and stifled what sounded like laughter, while the girls frowned at them in reproach. Tom heard these noises and saw these looks and he dropped his slanted gaze to the ground, then back to the horizon's horses.

James turned back to the Monster.

One thing was clear. It was dead. Tossed onto a bed of straw and crammed into the fractured remains of lidless apple box, James almost felt bad for it. This was nothing like the coffin that Greg Johnson's body had merited, nor was it as acceptable as the dirt and grass of the pet graves that James had seen in his lifetime. There was something rushed and makeshift about it, and James tried to convince himself that the Monster deserved it.

"It's got wings," said Willie.

"Look at its teeth," said Reggie.

Tom sighed again, and gazed out at the horses with what looked like a muddle of longing and hatred. James could imagine Tom leaping onto one of the animals and riding away. He could also imagine Tom taking a knife to the horses, or a club, or a gun. It seemed as if Tom himself could not decide what to do and so stood there, sweating, fists in pockets, somehow set apart from the unimpressed teenagers who gathered only a few feet away.

"Guy named Mel Herman ever come here?" asked Reggie. Tom shrugged and nodded, and the boys were not surprised. Mel's roving feet surely would have brought him to Tom's months ago.

James squatted down, brought his face closer to the Monster, sniffed it.

"What are you going to do with it?" he asked.

"Gonna mount it," Tom said instantly. "You know, like a deer head? Tack it to some stained wood, something real classy, maybe hang it up in the barn? Then make up a sign, put it out on the road. Maybe put some advertisements in the paper in Monroeville. Course, I'll have to clean up the barn. That ought to take a while. It's so hot in there, there's no ventilation. You guys ever want to make a couple bucks, you let me know. I got some pitchforks, you can clear out all that hay for me, huh?"

Tom's voice was prouder now, and though he spoke at the boys, his voice was aimed at the teenagers. After a moment, he kicked at a clump of weeds. "I got to get something from this," he murmured. "It's unusual. It's great. Nobody out there's seen anything like it, I bet."

Fifteen minutes were spent staring at the thing and pointing out its various attributes. Tom drifted toward the barn, where six or seven mangy cats nuzzled his ankles. Willie moved away and sat alone in the shadow of the silo. Reggie gravitated to the teenagers and began speaking to them in an artificially lowered voice. James alone remained hunched over the Monster, knees shaking, forehead pinched, back smarting. He tried to imagine this thing alive, its brittle bones lashed with muscle and covered with fur or scales or feathers, or some combination of all three, but as hard as he tried he could not do it. The Monster seemed like something that had always been dead, something stillborn into an apple box, packed unceremoniously into a crate, and suffocated in an attic for a hundred years. There was no life here.

When it came time to go, James had to call Reggie five or six times before Reggie rolled his eyes at the teenagers and nodded goodbye. He bumped shoulders with James as they joined in step at the mouth of the path.

James felt like someone should say something. "I don't know what kind of thing has teeth like that," he offered.

"Or wings like that," Willie added.

"You guys aren't going to believe this," said Reggie, his voice popping with the electricity that teenagers always provided him. "You know what they're planning to do? The big kids? You'll never guess what they're planning to do."

James did not look at him and did not answer. He prayed for Willie to stay quiet too.

"What?" asked Willie.

Reggie licked his lips and left them glistening with saliva.

"They're going to steal it."

James prayed for silence.

"Really?" asked Willie.

"Yeah," said Reggie. "But guess who's going to steal it first."

Cut Down

The next day, the boys decided to build a pulley system to get Willie up into the tree house, but were distracted by a dog that kept pacing around the trees behind the house. It watched them with black eyes and pawed the dirt, feigning approach before returning to shadow.

Willie disappeared inside and came back with binoculars and reported to the boys that the dog was fat. Reggie wrenched away the lens and planted it to his own eyes. "You can't use these with one hand," he muttered as he searched for the dog, found it, then adjusted some rings on the eyepieces.

"It's going to have puppies," he said.

They returned to work. Their tools included a hammer, a nest of nails, a length of rope, and a red metal pulley that Reggie had miraculously plucked from a trash can just down the street. Reggie did not usually poke through people's trash—like most boys, he preferred the epic solitude of the junkyard—but for reasons unknown he was compelled to lift that lid, and when he held up the rusty metal gear, James knew just what to do with it.

"There's a branch just above the roof," said James. "You can't see it, but I know it's there."

So he and Reggie scrambled up the steps, then up the side of the tree house itself, impressing themselves with their climbing abilities, then challenging each other with every daring leap and grip. Reggie reached the top of the tree house first, and when James joined him moments later they grinned at each other, chests heaving, as they brushed the crumbled bark from their elbows and knees. Reggie complimented James on a notable piece of footwork, and James insisted that he had no idea how Reggie had hurdled so quickly over the rooftop.

"I don't know either," said Reggie, and they both laughed.

They spent a few minutes scanning the distance, pointing out any truck that looked capable of murder. Then they remembered why they were up there and they both went flat on their tummies and snaked their bodies along the roof until their chins poked over the edge. Willie was far below, spinning in the grass. Reggie lowered a series of spit globs, at first taking care not to hit Willie, then hedging closer and closer. After two direct hits went unnoticed, Reggie shouted. "Hey, moron!"

Willie stopped spinning, then swayed in place, dizzy. His lone hand grasped at the air. He looked up at his friends and smiled. Then he reached down into the grass and held up the pulley. "You guys forgot the pulley," he said.

The trip down was easier—they dropped through the rectangular opening in the tree house roof, then took the steps by twos before leaping off with five or six feet still to go. Soon they were loading their pockets with nails and experimenting with ways to attach themselves with hammer, pulley, and rope.

"Dog's back," Willie said.

The animal was closer now, just across the yard, marching in place and sniffing the grass but never taking her eyes off them. She was black and white and shaggy with a hairy tail that brushed the ground. Dried mud caked her feet and her belly was distended. Six teats hung low, shiny and red.

"Pooch is probably thirsty," said Willie. "C'mere, pooch."

"Leave it alone," said Reggie.

"Poochie, poochie," said Willie, holding out his hand and making kissing sounds.

"Leave the stupid thing alone!" shouted Reggie. Willie and James looked at him in surprise. Reggie cast his eyes downward, found some nails, and slid them into his pocket. "That dog's going to have babies and you don't want it to have them here, believe me."

Willie grinned. "Puppies are cute."

Reggie picked up the hammer, tested its weight.

"My mom grew up on a farm and says that sometimes baby cows get stuck trying to get born and there are only two things you can do," said Reggie. "You can rip apart that baby cow while it's still in there, and take it out piece by piece, or you can cut the momma cow in half and save the baby. It's one or the other."

Reggie reared back and his arm whistled through air, and a nail struck a tree near the dog. The dog flinched, and sniffed, but did not run away. Reggie tossed another. It bounced off the animal's back. The dog's back legs skittered and it wheeled around, looking sharply about and flattening its ears.

"What are you doing?" cried Willie. "Knock it off! That's mean!"

Reggie threw another nail that fell short and lost itself in the grass.

"You don't want those puppies born here," said Reggie, not looking at Willie while he took aim with another nail.

"Hey!" said Willie. He moved toward Reggie. Another nail flew and rang off the top of the fence.

"It has those puppies here and they won't ever leave, ever," Reggie said. He leaned back to throw but Willie was now in his way, his face red, his lips drawn from the metal that laced through his teeth.

"Knock it off," said Willie.

"I'm doing you a favor," said Reggie.

"I know you are," said Willie.

"Not with the tree house, dummy," said Reggie, taking an easy step around Willie, and in the same motion transferring a nail to his throwing hand.

Willie spun and ran at the dog, shouting, "Go away, girl! Go away! Go away!" The animal shrank back, muscles defining themselves inside fur. Reggie threw another nail. It missed Willie's head by inches, and James gasped—he could too clearly imagine a nail lodging in Willie's eye, the bad luck of his life continuing.

But all James said was "Hey," and he was appalled at how weak it sounded. Why wasn't he moving to help Willie? Why was he just standing there? For some reason all he could think of was his parents.

The dog drew itself even lower and then slunk away in haste, its belly audibly rushing through the weeds. Willie stopped chasing it and then Reggie stopped, too. There was a long moment filled with sound—birds, insects, cars, sprinklers, lawn mowers. Finally Reggie picked up the pulley, hooked it to a belt loop, shouldered past James, and started up the tree.

"So I got a plan for getting the Monster," said Reggie as he climbed, "before the big kids or Mel Herman or anyone else gets to it. I'd tell you guys if you ever shut up for a second." Neither boy responded and the proposal died. The next sound from Reggie was the hammering of a nail into live wood.

Only now it was too late. Their inspiration had run off through the weeds with a thirsty, pregnant dog. This was work now, nothing else, and therefore the project was doomed.

It was not for lack of effort. Both Reggie and James shimmied up the tree dozens of times. They each took turns fastening the pulley to the first branch, gave up, then tried other branches, higher branches, thicker branches. When the pulley at last held, it was the rope that failed them, sliding from the pulley time after time. After a while, Mr. Van Allen stepped out onto the doorstep, perhaps drawn by the absence of conversation, and stood with his hands on the railing, his robe tied loosely around his waist.

His presence demanded a demonstration, but it was a clumsy, humiliating scene. The pulley shook, the rope slithered away, and James was reminded of Greg Johnson's funeral—those pulleys hadn't worked either. The boys attached the two-by-four that was to serve as Willie's seat, but when attempting to sit on it the best he could do was to lock his leg muscles in a squat while pretending the seat was not spinning uselessly beneath him. His friends' hands were all over him, steadying his back, lowering his butt, clasping his hand over the rope, then repositioning it, then repositioning his hand again and burning it when they moved it too quickly. Willie felt embarrassed for himself but also for his friends, and the more they all touched each other the more implicated they became in this extravagant, monumental failure.

Mr. Van Allen said nothing as his son lost balance and flopped to the ground, the rope spilling from the tree and falling in a pile on Willie's lap, his two friends collapsed around him, their elbows pink, their knees green, their eyes searching desperately for something that wasn't their fault.

I Am a Pawn

It rained for three days and everyone was excited until they stepped outside. The rain was hot.

Willie was sent out for milk and butter and eggs, no matter that it was late in the day and spitting liquid. He moved slowly, relishing this rare solo venture. It had come unexpectedly. Willie's mother had put on her shoes—the right one first, and then, much later, the left—and slung her purse over her shoulder and declared she was going to the store. Then she stood at the screen door for a long time, her hands at her sides, breathing slowly and watching the occasional raindrop explode on the sidewalk. Willie saw this happen too often: loud, busy preparations for some out-of-the-house errand that ended at the front door, as if his mother did not know how to release the lock or was afraid of what she would find beyond, or who would find her. Finally she repositioned herself and asked if Willie would like to go get some milk and butter and eggs.

He hopped up and thrust out his stump and she pinned the shirt's armhole in place so that the rain would not dampen the bandages, and then she opened his palm and unfolded into it dollar bills. "You be careful," she told him in a labored whisper, her eyes brimming with tears, and she hugged him forcefully as he wriggled to be set free. He stuffed the bills in his front pocket and strode out the front door, the wad of cash feeling thick and important against his hip. As he bolted down the front steps, he heard behind him a gasp from his mother, as if she too were thrilled and astonished by his velocity.

It was difficult for Willie to remember a time when he had gone out alone without incident. Once he had chipped a tooth on a parking meter. Another time he had become caught in a snowdrift until a mailman answered his cries. Yet another time he had been hit by a truck and lost his left arm.

This time he stuck to roads he knew and aimed himself along familiar landmarks: the Harper family tire swing, the tennis courts, the electrical cage with signs warning him to KEEP OUT, HIGH VOLTAGE. Then he was there, pushing through the door, goose-pimpling in the refrigerated aisle, sloshing around jugs of milk, attempting to gauge their comparative worth. Butter was easy— he grabbed the first package he saw. Eggs on the other hand involved lengthy deliberation, for Willie was not satisfied until each egg was lifted, rotated, and inspected for hairline cracks.

He had wrangled himself a cart, but on the way to the register ran into trouble. With only a single arm to guide it, the cart bore heavily to the left and Willie found himself tracing one, then two, then three ever-widening circles, and with each orbit he felt more eyes fall upon him. Still he wrenched and shoved and kicked, and tried to muscle the cart into a checkout lane, until a man in an apron came over and plucked the three grocery items from the cart. The man smiled at Willie, as if to assure him that he had made a valiant effort, but Willie knew a failure when he saw one and so avoided the man's face, kept his eyes on the food.

Willie left the store with change rattling in his front pocket, and though he was weighed down by groceries he felt quicker and lighter, overjoyed to leave behind the store, that bastard cart, the meddling men in aprons and the women ignoring their shopping lists. The paper sack he clutched marked him as someone not just winding his aimless way through the streets like Mel Herman. No, Willie Van Allen was *working*. He felt wonderful, and went down a wrong street on purpose.

Then he became fascinated with the way the rain darkened the brown paper sack and how the patterns expanded–miserly faces swelled into obesity, branches grew root systems, stars joined to create planets–and when he finally remembered to look up it was too late. He was lost. The rain slopped against his neck and he stood there, letting his new failure fully soak.

The houses looked friendlier down one street, so he went that way. A sprinkler circulated pointlessly in the rain and Willie stepped out of its spray, briefly onto the road. He heard tires skimming though wet pavement. He rushed back to the curb, regripped the humid sack.

A truck rolled past and Willie eyed it warily.

When the truck reached the far street, it turned right. When Willie reached the same intersection he turned left. Something was happening to the paper sack; it felt gummy. He felt a wave of panic and snuggled it deeper into his armpit. He looked at a house and saw a face in a window, a child. Willie became aware of his stump in a way he hadn't before. He looked away from the child. Water dripped from his long nose. There was a squish in his socks. He felt his bandages getting wet and wondered what that meant–his mother had warned him against it so many different times. He searched this way and that for orientation, but everything was as smeared as a Mel Herman painting, and for a moment Willie wondered if the world through Mel's eyes was always this murky and upsetting.

From the corner of his eye he saw the truck again. The same truck as before, he was almost positive. It sat in the middle of the road, engine humming, gray smoke rolling between its back tires. Willie gripped his grocery sack and his fingernails slid right through the paper. The jug of milk was warm and perspiring. His mother would not approve.

The truck moved, then its taillights went red and it paused, as hesitant as the pregnant dog skulking around Willie's house. Willie stared straight ahead. He heard the truck slither away. It would circle around and come back again, he knew it.

Willie turned left. The bottom of the bag parted and the milk jug hit the sidewalk. The eggs and butter tried to slip through too, but Willie folded up his body and managed to pin the items against him. He set everything down on the ground and opened the eggs to evaluate the damage. Two broken that he could see. He stood up and watched the rain drum patiently upon the open eggs, the overturned milk jug, the package of butter. It was an odd sight and for a moment he was transfixed.

There was no way he could get everything home without the sack. He grabbed the wet butter, shoved it into his underwear, and picked up the heavy milk jug by the handle. There were no eggs, that's what he would say. The store was out of eggs. What happened to the rest of the money, then? Willie scrunched his forehead and felt rain forge new routes down his temples.

He turned again because it felt like progress. He came upon the same lawn sprinkler he had dodged earlier and this time he walked right through it. He thought about going straight at the intersection. He wondered how far the road extended. He thought about the long, windy path that led to Tom and the thing in the apple box. Perhaps there was a resting spot at the end of this road, too.

He set the milk jug within the wet branches of a shrub. Maybe later he could find it again, present it to his mother, make amends.

He did not notice the rain pick up until his sneakered foot swept through a puddle and the water fanned through the air. Now he staggered—he had hurt his toe. He crossed one intersection, another. He heard an engine somewhere nearby, and he sped through yet another intersection, his toe throbbing. He began to limp. The package of butter fell from his pants leg and he left it. He felt himself mumbling and tried to stop it but the words kept coming, strange sentences that he had invented for homework, stranger sentences that he had invented at home for no reason at all, nonsensical phrases that stood for coniferous-deciduous or Indian-Arctic-Atlantic-Pacific or molar-premolar-incisor-canine or Mercury-Venus-Earth-Mars-Jupiter-Saturn-Uranus-Neptune-Pluto.

At the following intersection he saw a truck, maybe the same color as the one he'd seen earlier, which was maybe the same color as the one that struck him several months ago, he couldn't remember, not now, not with these sentences rattling through his brain. He staggered onward and his limp reminded him of how his father walked these days, as if he were constantly butting invisible obstacles with his pajama-clad knees. Sometimes his father even winced, as if the pain of these collisions were real.

His father even walked that way outside, sometimes clutching his beer with both hands as if that might steady him, and sometimes it did. Other times the alcohol made things worse and he would end up wandering the backyard gripping the fence. Other times he would tuck his beer into the waistband of his pants and push the lawn mower in meandering ovals until his limp worked itself out. The lawn was mostly dirt now, except for below the tree house where the grass was lush and soft—it had not been mowed in months.

Willie stomped through a puddle, then skipped, trying to keep off his sore toe. *Lust-gluttony-avarice-sloth-wrath-envy-pride.* He remembered what the boys said at the junkball field, that they heard Willie's father roamed the town at night, sometimes in his robe, sometimes with dirty knees, sometimes bloodied. Now Willie wondered if it might be true. After all, here *he* was, wandering in the rain on some street he'd never seen before, inappropriately clothed and limping, like father, like son. He felt a rush of stubborn pride for his father. He pictured him— his robe, his beer, his maybe-dirty knees, his maybe-bloodied body—and Willie hastened to match his own limp to the one he'd memorized from his dad: *diamonds-clubs-hearts-spades.*

Now when Willie heard tires on a neighboring street splitting the rain in two, he felt fright, real fright. *Asia-Antarctica-Europe-Africa-North-America-South-America-*

Australia: he limped faster. His father limped alongside him, or so Willie imagined, but instead of feeling safer he felt exposed and dissected like a science-class insect, pinned down with parts labeled—Missing Arm, Crooked Teeth, Elephant Ears, Long Nose. So he kept moving, because at the end of the road could be anything, *anything,* and if it was an apple box and a crate he was more than ready to be packed away in a warm attic corner, away from eyes, safe from the rain.

He ran faster and louder, and the truck, too: louder, faster. He urged himself on, out loud and with strange sentences indicating the treble clef notes, the bass clef, the first five books of the Bible, and the reedy sound of his own panicked voice revealed everything about him: he was a short, flimsy, worthless kid. Maybe the truck coming up behind him was a killer, maybe it wasn't; maybe it was the stupid Johnsons, doing their stupid daily patrol. This possibility was the most harrowing. Because if concerned parents were inside the approaching vehicle, they would see him running and they would pull over to the side of the road and ask what was wrong, dear? And he would have to keep running, for if he turned around he'd see his reflection in the passenger window: a boy with one arm, carrying no food at all, soaked to the bone, shivering and small—not small, tiny!—and whether he liked it or not they were going to scoop him up in their arms, drag him kicking into the vehicle, and drive him straight home, touching him all over like Reggie and James had touched him when the tree house pulley collapsed. He would not accept such contact, not now, not again, not ever.

When he saw the Harper family tire swing and therefore the way home, he coughed up more words: "I smell meat." There it was, home, and he would have to explain the missing money and food. But he would not tell the truth. The truth was something he had dropped along with the milk and butter and eggs. The truth was something for helpless children, and from here on it would be a thing foreign to him, he would see to it, he made himself promise. This thing that just happened, this lost errand, this maybe-pursuit, it was his and he would keep it. He would not tell anyone.

My Panic Inches Closer

"Reggie."

"What?"

"You think he'll be mad?"

"Who, Willie?"

"Yeah."

Reggie considered it. "I guess it doesn't really matter. He's never going to know we're up here."

"Yeah, but it's his tree house."

"It *was* his tree house. He can't own it anymore, James, you know why? Because you can't own something you can't touch. Just like you can't own the sun and I can't own the moon. Look, we tried. That pulley idea of yours was great. But face it. He'll never see the inside of this thing again. He's probably already forgot what it looks like."

"Maybe we should try again. We could lift him, maybe. If we tried together, you think?"

"It's impossible. Remember how hard it was getting him through the school window? I thought he was going to kill himself. No way we'd ever get him all the way up here. He'd fall and break his neck. And then we'd be in real trouble."

There was silence for a while. It was late, well past curfew, something that still made James nervous when he thought of his folks noticing the toll of the grand-father clock, which they would any minute now, any second, and the two boys lay on their backs on the wooden floor of Willie Van Allen's tree house. Their heads almost touched so that they could both stare through the rectangle Mr. Van Allen had cut from the roof long ago. There were tree leaves above, blacker even than the night, and then, above those, the shimmering pinpoints of stars.

On the wall before them hung the oversize Mel Herman painting they had stolen from the school. It had been there for weeks and both boys had spent much time, together and alone, studying its infinite detail. Reggie said it looked like blueprints. James kept return-ing to the tiny vehicle running over a tiny person, and for that reason insisted the painting must be a map. If they could just decipher it, he said, it could lead them somewhere important. "To Mel's house," said Reggie, his dark eyes flashing, although that was not what James meant.

From his spot on the floor James looked from the painting to the dark sky above and breathed deeply. Reggie had a point. The tree house *was* pretty high. At night even he and Reggie had to be cautious when they climbed.

"Well, we at least should've told him we're borrowing it," said James.

"What, you just want to make him feel bad?" said Reggie. "It's better this way. It's better if we just sneak in after his parents have locked the doors and tucked him into bed."

"He's not asleep yet, it's not that late," said James.

"Of course he's not sleeping." Reggie sighed. "He's sitting around staring at his Lincoln Logs or telling Softie how crummy it is to have one arm."

"Shh."

"Stop worrying," Reggie said. "He sure as hell can't hear us. They have their fans on full-blast because the dummies keep all their windows locked. I guess they think . . ."

He trailed off.

"They think what?" asked James.

James felt Reggie shrug.

"You don't think a truck could break through a house, do you?" Reggie asked.

James considered it for a moment. It was an unpleasant thought.

"No," James said. "I doubt it." He paused. "I hope not."

"Yeah," said Reggie. "No kidding."

A vehicle rumbled past on the road. The floorboards vibrated. Mel Herman's painting trembled, took on brief new meanings, then was still. James shivered.

"Anyway," Reggie said, "let's face it. It's probably good that Willie's locked in. He's safer down there. Indoors, I mean. He doesn't really belong out here with us anymore."

James frowned into the night sky. "But it's not the same without him."

"Of course it's not the same," said Reggie. "But *he's* not the same either. Neither are you. Me neither. Nothing's ever the same, James. Kids get older. Kids change. Some kids get in accidents and lose their arms. What are you going to do, cry about it? You just have to go ahead and get older."

James imagined Willie, somewhere below them, lying on his bed, holding Softie to his cheek with his one arm. James inhaled and held his breath, feeling his rib cage expand his chest and letting the night air fill his body until he felt heavy and powerful. He stretched against the floorboards and found that he could feel the end of the tree house with his toes—he was getting taller.

"We can still hang out with him," Reggie said. "I have no problem with that. But some things we'll have to do without him. Sometimes we'll have to leave him behind."

James exhaled and felt the muscles in his chest tingle. He blinked his eyes and thought that the night looked like a black mirror, and those two stars right there were his own eyes reflecting back at him. He felt as big as the sky.

For some reason, the idea of leaving Willie behind was exciting. It reminded James of picking teams in gym class–you had to choose the best players if you wanted to win. Sure, excluding Willie made James feel merciless. It also made him feel like a grown-up, like someone forced to make tough choices and live with them. It did feel awkward having these thoughts while lying inside Willie's own tree house, where the three of them had spent so many hours reading comic books, dropping tiny green paratroopers, and whispering into the dead of night while tucked into side-by-side sleeping bags.

"Like my plan for getting the Monster, for instance," Reggie was saying. "Willie can't come with us for that. For a million reasons. Can't you just picture it?"

James hesitated. He had planned on convincing Reggie that stealing the Monster was a bad idea. But tonight James didn't want to–an exhilarating new courage stirred within him. Steal the Monster? Why not? There was a part of him that enjoyed imagining his parents pacing the floor at home, fretting about his safety. Sometimes disobedience felt good and he wanted to give himself over to it, become someone who ate danger and breathed risk like Reggie Fielder.

"What do you think they'll do to him?" Reggie asked.

James blinked.

"Who?"

"The guy. You know, the guy with the silver truck. What'll they do when they catch him?"

James paused. "What do *you* think?" he asked.

"Jail. Probably for a long time. If they can prove he did it, if they can prove he had a silver truck and that it was the same kind that hit Willie and Greg? Then maybe even the death penalty."

James listened to their breathing for a while before replying. Mel's painting was barely visible in the darkness, but James knew it well enough now to know that Mel's world was not made of straight lines and bright colors—it was sharp-toothed, mystifying, and painful.

"I think it might be worse than the death penalty," James said softly. "I've heard that sometimes when a bunch of grown-ups get real mad at once, they do illegal things and get away with it, because the cops can't throw all the grown-ups in jail at the same time, it's just impossible. So I think if they catch the guy, there's a good chance that all the grown-ups in town will get together and go to wherever they're keeping him—at the jail or wherever—and then they'll drag him out of there. He'll try to get away but there will be too many of them. Then they'll take the guy somewhere where there's nobody around to watch, like maybe the woods or some farmer's field. And then they'll do something bad to him."

"Like how bad?" asked Reggie. "You mean kill him?"

James could not keep away the terrible thoughts. He burned with a fire kindled by Mel Herman's canvas and fanned by past-curfew air.

"Maybe worse," he said. "Maybe worse than murder, because the guy hurt and killed kids. Grown-ups get real crazy about kids. And so maybe they'll tear his arm off. You know, for justice. To make it fair. Because Willie lost his arm. Maybe they just tear this guy's arm off."

"Jesus," said Reggie.

"And then maybe they keep going. Because I've heard that once grown-ups start something like this, they can't get themselves to stop. They get like a pack of wolves, like they're wolves tearing apart a, a . . ."

"Caribou?"

"Right," said James. "And once they've tasted the meat they just can't stop. Grown-ups don't even like police and judges and stuff. Because grown-ups don't like being told what to do. I mean, you know—they're *grown-ups*. And so maybe they keep going."

Reggie swallowed. "Keep going how?"

James shrugged.

"After they pull off his arm," said James, "then maybe they pull off his other arm. Then maybe they take an ax and chop off his legs. Then they look at him on the ground with no arms and no legs and they laugh at him when he tries to roll away. But maybe they don't even stop there."

"Jesus."

"Maybe they don't want this guy even *looking* at kids anymore. So they poke out his eyes. And then they don't want him tasting good things anymore, either, so they cut off his tongue. And then someone says they better go ahead and cut off his nose, too, because there's all sorts of good smells in the world, like hot chocolate and mowed grass."

"Jesus."

"And then they probably just leave him there, without legs or arms or eyes or a face, just sort of rocking back and forth in the grass like a little baby. But they don't kill him because they want him to think about what he's done, about how he killed that one kid and tore off that other kid's arm—those poor little kids. And the guy lies there with bugs all over him and rats chewing off his skin. He can't cry because he's got no eyes and can't yell for help because he's got no tongue. You know how long it takes to die from starvation?"

"Nuh-uh."

"A really long time."

The stars above were no longer friendly, they were the points of a million knives poised to stab. Beneath this terror, they stared at Mel Herman's distorted map—the tiny vehicle, the tiny dead person, the hundreds of other scenes of possible violence—and they thought about the killer, perhaps also located somewhere on Mel's map, disemboweled, alone, and dying. Finally Reggie spoke, startling James.

"Serves him *right*," he growled.

Many Vanish Entirely, Many Just Soak Up New Pains

Willie could not come out. Ever since losing the milk, butter, and eggs, and then returning two hours late from seeing the Monster, he was allowed only to speak through the latched screen door, mumbling stuff about his parents and how they were trying to spend more time with him. To James this seemed like a lie; he could see Mrs. Van Allen troubling the appliances and chairs and curtains as she always did, and Mr. Van Allen in the same wrinkled pajamas contemplating what could be the same gutted newspaper. James understood the real reason: the

Van Allens no longer trusted the boys, any of them—not James, not Reggie, not even Willie.

But Willie was twelve—he couldn't stay in there forever, and everyone knew it. Outings were therefore planned, as much as a week in advance and only after a relentless series of parent-to-parent phone calls. James felt a new, uncomfortable pressure as he walked up the Van Allen steps and knocked on the door.

From inside sang Mrs. Van Allen's voice: "Come in, James, and lock the door behind you."

This was unusual. The door was never unlocked. James pulled it open carefully and stepped inside. He had a sudden sensation that Mr. Van Allen was looming behind him, and James spun around expecting bloodshot eyes, putty skin, and foamy lips, but there was nothing there but a rack on the wall with a fedora and a set of keys.

"You didn't lock the door."

Yes, it was Mr. Van Allen's voice, but coming from a safe distance away, over at the kitchen table, right where he ought to be. James noted that the absence of sound that forewarned an unlocked door was something Mr. Van Allen knew by heart. James hurried back and with nervous, fumbling fingers learned how to draw the lock.

"Over here!" called Willie.

Grateful to escape the presence of Mr. Van Allen, James hastened to the living room. He was around the corner in seconds, but stopped at the sight of exposed flesh.

Willie's shirt was off and his stump was naked. It was a shocking white, whiter even than the rest of Willie's chest and upper arms, and the tip of it was a flushed pink. The skin around the nub was snarled into a grimace as if the surgeon had twisted shut the wound like a bag of bread.

Mrs. Van Allen had one arm around Willie's back and the other was playfully poking at the twitching stump with a cloth. For a moment, James was caught up: the laughter, the comfortable touches between mother and son, the kind of contact James had not shared with his own parents for a number of years. But the longing went away. There was nothing funny about a malformed lump of flesh where an arm used to be, so why were they laughing? Willie would one day grow up and become Mr. William Van Allen and he still wouldn't have a left arm. Watching Willie's mother pin up his sleeve was like watching a mommy fastening her baby's diaper. It offended James; maybe Reggie had been right about Willie. They couldn't spend the rest of the summer babysitting, if that's what it really was.

Reggie had pointed out scars all his life—on the faces of carnival workers, on the hands of fishermen—and seemed to long after them as a sign of manhood. James, however, knew of the mark on his mother's lip, and therefore knew that sometimes scars were evidence only of a body's refusal to heal. James remembered a strange moment, many years ago, when Call-Me-Kay had lifted the hem of her blouse and pushed down the waist of her skirt to show the boys a thin white scar somehow related to Reggie's birth. Reggie had demanded she put it away, and looked as if he wanted to thrust his hands into that old wound and reopen it, rip her in half. It would not have made much difference, as it was but one of Ms. Fielder's many scars: cigarette burns, neglected ear piercings, a white semicircle on her temple where an unskilled doctor had stitched a cut. With so many old wounds to her credit, Reggie's mother was tougher than all three boys put together. This embarrassed James, and the next time she offered to show them her belly scar, he joined Reggie in saying no.

Watching Mrs. Van Allen finish up Willie's sleeve, and hearing the whir of the fan that spun inches from Mr. Van Allen's face, James realized that the Van Allens were nothing but scar, and lived in a wound so big you could no longer see it. This thought scared him. If life was an accumulation of scars that told your story better than any stupid scrapbook, Willie needed to slow down. His scarring was too great for someone his age, and his book was running out of pages.

James was uncomfortable; he wanted to leave. He turned aside and examined the first thing he saw, an empty aquarium.

"I've been practicing," said Willie. "Wanna hear?"

James wrinkled his nose at the sour smell of the scum lining the aquarium glass. "Sure," he said, wishing that Mr. Van Allen had kept him locked outside. "Go ahead."

Willie screwed up his face into a knot that looked like

the tip of his stump, and shouted in a high-pitched voice, "Steeeeeee-riiiiike threeeeee! Youuuuuuuu're outta there!"

James had to hand it to Willie. Instead of getting down about it, like James figured *he* would if *his* arm got squashed under a truck, Willie enthusiastically dove into his new role of umpire-for-life. All the way to the junkball field, Willie yelled crazy ump garbage like, "Baaaaaaaaaall four!" and "Plaaaaaaaaaaay baaaaaaaaaa-aaall!" Reggie, who had joined them without a word, glanced at James over Willie's head. He said nothing, but James got the message: Reggie was putting up with Willie, but just barely.

When they got to the field, five other boys were already there. They divided into teams and went at it. Before one inning was through, the boys' shirts were shaded with sweat. They licked their salty chins and pounded their chapped fists into the cracked leather of secondhand gloves. Between pitches, the fielders shouted to throw the batter off-rhythm. But when the batter swung the only noise was the trill of crickets slinging themselves through outfield grass.

Everyone agreed it was good to have an umpire. Unfortunately, Willie was neither skilled nor fair. No matter how good the pitch was to James or Reggie, Willie refused to call a strike. To compensate James and Reggie started swinging at every terrible pitch that came their way.

Mel Herman showed up at the top of the second.

Despite the heat, he still wore his large black shirt, but had made one concession to the blazing heat: his pants were cut off at the knee. All chatter from the boys on the field died, and for a moment they sweated in silence.

"I'm here, nutballs," Mel said.

"We already got a game," said Reggie, glancing at James and Willie.

Mel Herman counted the players, the sun blasting off his thick, taped-up glasses.

"You jackasses are uneven!" he said. "Sweet blessed lord, good thing I'm here."

Reggie had nothing to say to that—it was true. So Mel joined the other team and proceeded to smack the hell out of the ball. It was annoying for everyone, as it meant continual halts in play as they tried to locate the ball among the junked cars in right field or under the chain-link fence in left-center. After he strolled across home plate, Mel just stood there watching the hapless outfielders, not happy, not angry, not offering help, nothing.

In the fifth inning, a kid threw pitches in the dirt so Mel couldn't hit them. After four straight mud balls, a red color poured up from Mel's collar and his jaw muscles pulsed beneath the skin. He took first base, but from then on the pitcher couldn't concentrate—he had to keep making sure that Mel was not charging him, claws outstretched, bent on murder. That was the first and last time anyone tried to walk Mel Herman.

When Reggie came to bat, he whispered to Willie.

"We gotta follow him."

Willie frowned. "Who? Where?"

"Mel. To where he lives."

"How come?"

Reggie wiped the sweat off of his forehead with his sleeve. "To see what kind of truck his family has, stupid."

"Oh," said Willie, squatting in the umpire stance. He squinted at Mel, who was picking his nose near second base. His glasses were full with sun and his eyes were great bright blotches. Willie chewed on his lip. Maybe Mel wasn't just some crazy painter who occasionally threw gum in your hair. Could it be he was something much worse?

The game broke up in the early afternoon. A couple of boys were late for swimming lessons, and it was getting way too hot. Besides, the score was 16–2, and Mel was the only one doing any scoring.

"Why do you cockenheimers want to quit?" Mel asked the three friends as they gathered their stuff. He posed the question as if he honestly didn't know.

"We have to go home," said Reggie, picking up his glove and bat. James and Willie stayed close and busied themselves with slapping the dust from their clothes.

"I vote we keep playing," said Mel.

"Yeah, well, we can't," said Reggie.

"I was having a fine time with you paraplegics."

"I could tell," said Reggie.

Mel's face was as empty as a clean chalkboard. He regarded the boys for a moment.

"What else you paraplegics like to do?"

"We don't like to do anything," said Reggie. "Come on, guys, let's go."

They started away, leaving Mel booting around the hubcap that served as third base. James could feel Mel's presence behind them, and winced each time the hubcap rang. They were a good distance away when Mel called out.

"You're lucky I don't beat in your paraplegic heads," he said.

Reggie's eyes gleamed. There it was. That old Mel Herman temper. See how it flared up? See? This creep was capable of anything. James and Willie looked at each other and walked faster.

After they turned the corner, Reggie pulled the three of them into a gutted, upside-down car. They got on their hands and knees and huddled inside, their foreheads wedged against the leather seats, dangling seatbelts knocking against their noses.

"We'll hide here," Reggie whispered. "Be quiet. After he goes by, we follow him."

Reggie gripped the baseball bat hard.

* * *

They trailed Mel Herman for almost an hour. They dodged behind newspaper kiosks and parked cars, and ended up in vaudevillian tangles when one of them stopped too abruptly. It was so bright their eyes ached from squinting.

"Can't we stop for orange sodas?" asked Willie. "Sodas. *Orange* sodas. Wanna stop?"

Reggie paused, keeping one eye on Mel Herman, who lumbered along like a bear maybe a block farther up the road. Willie pointed with his single arm to a hand-written sign that shouted: COLD DRINKS.

Reggie kept focus upon the steadily shrinking Mel.

"No," Reggie said. "We only got one shot at this. We can't let him out of our sight."

He charged on. After an unhappy moment, James and Willie followed.

They were in a part of town they'd never seen before—beyond the abandoned public swimming pool, out of sight of the MacArthur Building, across the railroad tracks, through the Leisure Estates mobile home park, and down an alley crowded with overflowing trash bins, rusted stoves, and haphazard tangles of metal. James sensed a resemblance between these landmarks and the Mel Herman map hanging in the tree house. They were in Mel's world now and it scared him.

"What do we do if he sees us?" he asked.

Reggie shrugged, his sweaty face adopting the stubborn mug of a bulldog. "I'll do what I have to do."

"Yeah, but what's that?" asked James.

Reggie shrugged again. "What has to be done."

James worried that this could develop into another Leon Heller situation. A couple years back, a new kid arrived at their school. His name was Leon. He was a skinny kid with floppy blond hair, a long face, and a loose, goofy smile. He seemed all right. But Leon Heller had one fatal flaw: his eyelashes were too long. He had dark, curly lashes that looked like they belonged on a woman. When he started getting picked on, kids made up all kinds of excuses—"He stole my lunch" or "He keeps looking at me weird"—but James knew the real reason they tormented him. It was because of those eyelashes.

One day, on the school's south staircase, Leon shoved a kid named Jesse Dratch all the way down the stairs. Jesse landed with a gruesome crunch, then flopped onto his stomach and started screaming into the floor. Leon just walked away, leaving Jesse to writhe in pain until his reverberating din drew the teachers.

Or at least that's how the story went. No one James knew had actually *seen* the event. But plans went into action to punish Leon. James thought this was strange, because no one had paid much attention to Jesse before. But now the name Jesse Dratch was on every boy's lips— they must get their revenge for what that scoundrel Leon Heller did to their good, good friend Jesse Dratch.

Reggie spearheaded the plot. He passed around a note instructing all the boys in class to meet behind the kickball field at recess. At the meeting, Reggie did most of the talking. They'd have to corner Leon Heller somewhere, he said. They'd have to carry things with them, like baseball bats or tennis rackets or hockey sticks. They couldn't let that punk get away with something like this.

Reggie conducted several of these meetings, and while he talked he glared across the playground at Leon, who sat alone along the side of the school, talking to himself and smiling into the grass.

James had never seen Reggie get this excited about anything—and why was he so excited about beating up some new kid? James imagined all the boys circling around Leon Heller with their makeshift weapons and imagined how Leon would fight back but eventually lose. He wondered how long they would beat Leon, and how hard, and how much blood there would be. Mostly he wondered if Reggie would ever stop beating him— after all, it was Reggie's pet project and he might be sorry to see it end.

It was agreed to do it after school one Monday in November. To all the boys' surprise, Jesse Dratch returned to school that very day wearing a cast around his shoulder. He was clearly pleased at his hero's welcome. All the kids gathered around him, cheering and patting him on the back like he was their best friend in the world. Jesse looked confused but happy.

When somebody asked Jesse to describe how Leon had shoved him down the stairs, Jesse just shrugged and grinned. He explained how he had grabbed Leon's backpack and had lost his balance when Leon turned around. A few seconds later his collarbone was split in two.

James felt his body relax muscle by muscle. There would be no fight, no revenge, no blood, no suspensions. He looked at Reggie, expecting to see similar relief. But instead Reggie's face was red and trembling. He was *angry* that Leon was innocent. He was *furious* that his brutal plans were dissolving before his eyes. Perhaps his anger had something to do with the other boys in class and how rapidly they were remembering how to ignore him.

Today, as they trailed Mel Herman down a potholed stretch of pavement that baked heat upward like a stove, Reggie wore a similar expression of wrathful determination. James felt as if once more he was being led to violence he did not want, yet he could not stop his feet from following Reggie.

"We'll get in trouble if we hurt him," said James.

Reggie didn't flinch. "I'll cover for you guys. I'll say I did it by myself. Who's going to punish me, my mom?"

Broken glass scrunched beneath their sneakers.

"You maybe could get suspended for something like this, maybe," said James.

Reggie shrugged. "I doubt it. But even if you're right, I'll probably drop out in a few years anyway."

They kicked through a pile of pigeons, who barely waddled aside to let them pass.

"I just don't know what we're doing," said James, maybe to himself, "or where we're going."

"I do," Reggie snapped, ending the conversation. He pointed ahead. "We're going that way."

Let's Go and See
Why Everyone Prays

The sights they were familiar with receded until they recognized only particular groves of trees, and then those trees receded, too. They crossed Oleander Avenue, then a second length of train tracks that ripped across the cement landscape like a zipper, demolishing everything the boys were accustomed to—grass, leaves, birds, squirrels, playgrounds—and replacing them with the debris of a grown-up world: trash-filled gutters, rusted-out gas stations, and factories with silent black windows. James and Willie hoped that Reggie would remember the way home, and they all kept a lookout for trucks.

The boys had not spoken in what seemed like forever. Far ahead, moving at a constant pace, Mel Herman remained a fuzzy black dot. Occasionally James rubbed his face to make sure Mel wasn't just a piece of dirt caught in his eye.

When James first saw the motel, it looked like yet another squalid building ruined with peeling paint. In fact, he probably never would've noticed the motel at all if he hadn't heard Willie mumbling words under his breath.

". . . varancy?"

"Huh?" James asked him in a low voice.

Willie was staring at the motel sign, which read: VA AN Y. Two letters were missing and Willie could not resist the challenge.

"Valaney?" Willie said to himself. "Vapanry?"

James wrinkled his nose as they passed the motel. His family spent a week or two on vacation most summers—he'd seen the mountains, the ocean, the desert, the biggest city in the country, too—and they always stayed in fancy rooms with large-countered bathrooms and mints perched atop mounds of pillows. Never did they stay in a place like this one. James imagined the beds as dusty and stinking of feet. Still, as he looked it over, there was something that seemed familiar.

"Vacancy!" cried Willie softly, smiling in victory.

And then James figured it out. That car in the parking lot. It sure looked a lot like his father's car. As they passed, James looked harder. Was that their license plate number? He wasn't sure. Did their car have a dent in the rear fender? He couldn't remember.

Just beyond the car, in the motel window, someone parted the curtains and glanced up at the sky. James tried to see. Was it his dad? No—this person was smoking. This person was also a woman. James stared harder, but as he took his next step the sun threw a great bucket of light against the motel window, blinding James and making him look away. Yet he thought he had recognized the woman.

It had looked like Call-Me-Kay, Reggie's mother.

James stole a glance at Reggie, who charged down the sidewalk, eyes locked onto Mel Herman's back. James checked Willie, who was still whispering the word "vacancy," his braces glinting in the sun. No one else had seen her.

Was it really Reggie's mother? And was it really his father's car? A quick jolt of dread knifed down James's back—he remembered the morning after the school adventure, and how his father hadn't believed his fib about sleeping over at Reggie's house. Maybe that was it: together James's dad and Reggie's mom were uncovering the lie, and later there would be punishment for both boys. The only reason they were meeting in a motel was because James's mother disapproved of Ms. Fielder, and where else could two grown-ups gather in private? He tried to convince himself this was true, but he felt worse than he had all day. There were other reasons for two grown-ups to meet in a motel.

* * *

Mel Herman's house was low and small and clung desperately to a collapsed front porch. Alongside the front lawn was an even smaller one-car garage. Both buildings were painted strangely—brown predominated, but the trim was a hodgepodge of color so bright and unexpected that it looked like a flock of exotic birds preparing to fly.

The three of them gathered behind a warehouse directly across the street. The heat was painful and the tops of their ears burned. They wondered aloud in awed tones: Did Mel Herman walk this far to school every day? On foot? Didn't he own a bike? And what happened in winter? Did he walk that far through three feet of snow?

James felt sudden shame about their attempts to exclude Mel Herman from junkball. After all, if Mel walked over an hour just to reach the field, he must really love to play. James didn't like feeling sorry for Mel Herman. He started hoping that Mel's family *did* own a silver truck, one with a dented side door spattered with Willie's blood or a busted grill that still clutched tufts of Greg Johnson's hair. Because at this point—so far from home, so moist with heat, so weary beneath the threat of Reggie's baseball bat—it was just easier to continue hating him.

Mel ducked inside the front door and nothing happened for a while. Without warning, Reggie sailed across the street and James and Willie chased after, wincing at the loud clap of sneakers on pavement. Panting, they joined Reggie at the front of the garage. James looked across the small lawn, expecting a large, dark shape to bolt from the front door at any moment.

Reggie balanced on his tiptoes and tried to look through the garage window.

"What's in there?" asked James. "A truck?"

Reggie bared his teeth and stretched farther. He tried hopping and still came up short. Reggie set down his baseball bat, kneeled down, and opened his arms. Willie grumbled and stepped in. Reggie wrapped his arms around Willie's legs and lifted him, then carefully rotated so that Willie faced the garage window. James watched in horror. Now it really looked bad–they weren't just trailing him, they were peering into his garage! Any second now: Mel, charging from the house and the boys fleeing in naked terror. Possibly if they ran like mad they could make it back to the motel, where their parents, if they weren't too angry, would protect them.

"Oh wow," gasped Willie, looking inside the garage.

"What do you see?" Reggie demanded, struggling beneath Willie's weight.

"Wow," Willie said again.

Reggie lowered Willie to the ground, breathing hard.

"What?" Reggie hissed.

"What's in there?" James asked.

Willie blinked and looked surprised to see them.

Then a smile spread across his face.

"They got a scooter in there. I always wanted a scooter."

James exhaled and prickly sensations shot out through his fingertips. Without planning it, he laughed out loud.

Reggie's neck went red, and he glared at James. Then he turned that glare on Willie.

"You couldn't ride a scooter if you had one," he said. "How are you going to steer it? With one arm? That's pathetic."

Willie's smile faded.

"What do you mean?" he asked.

Reggie sneered. "What do you mean, what do I mean? I mean, some stuff you need two arms to do. Otherwise, you just screw it up and embarrass yourself."

"I wouldn't screw it up."

Reggie's laugh was short and loud. "Willie, you'd screw it up with *two* arms."

Willie paused, and seemed to give the moment uncharacteristic reflection. "You said I was pathetic."

"Well, if you try to do certain things you *will* be pathetic. You remember the tree house, don't you?"

"That wasn't my fault. You guys couldn't hook up the—"

"The what? The pulley? Why were we hooking it up in the first place, Willie? I mean, the whole *thing* is pathetic."

Willie squinted at Reggie.

"Why are you being so mean?" he asked.

James wished Reggie would shut up. This was tree

house talk, and it ought to stay between the two of them. These were not things Willie needed to hear, not ever, not even if they were true.

"You think I'm being mean? I'll tell you what I'm being, I'm being helpful," Reggie snapped. "Take a look at yourself. Do you have any idea how much of a drag you are? If we're running somewhere or climbing over something, you ever notice how much time we spend helping you keep up? I'm not being mean here—if I were you I'd listen. Because if you go around trying to do things like a normal boy, you're going to get made fun of. People are going to laugh at you. They're going to say mean things, and you know what? You're going to deserve it, because you should've known better."

"I am a normal boy," said Willie, though he did not sound so sure.

"You're not like the normal boys I know," said Reggie.

Willie looked squarely at Reggie. The scar on his neck seemed darker than usual.

Finally, Willie spoke. "You don't need two arms for a scooter."

And then, loud and sudden:

"You guys follow me?"

The three boys turned in unison and there he was, blotting out the sun and throwing them into shadow. In the next instant the boys saw Mel Herman in detail so exquisite it was painful: the downy hairs sprouting from his upper lip; the thin trail of scabs running down his calf;

the color of his shirt, which was no longer black, but instead a murk of stains and discolorations, blue, purple, red, brown, gray.

Mel spoke again and his mouth barely moved.

"You guys follow me?"

Each boy hoped the other might respond with something sharp and brilliant; instead their silence said everything. James watched as Mel silently wiped his palms on his shirt. Those hands, those large, filthy paws topped with jags of fingernails, were somehow responsible for all of those paintings lining the hallways of Polk Elementary, as well as that spectacular mess tacked up on the tree house wall.

Bees buzzed about them; it was the only sound. The hot air hung heavy, pinning the boys to the cement.

Reggie dropped down and picked up the bat.

It must have seemed to Reggie that this was the smart thing to do—if Mel attacked, they would need a defense. To James it was a blunt and hasty declaration of war, and revealed exactly what the boys thought of Mel Herman: he was an animal and this is how animals were beaten. James wanted no part of this, but it was far too late to say so.

Mel's eyes dipped to look at the baseball bat, then slowly crawled over each boy's face. He did not appear angry or scared, only tired. For a moment James thought Mel might just bow his head and walk away.

But then Mel's bottom jaw chomped at his lip, his shoulders broadened as if his oversized shirt concealed mighty wings, and all of a sudden he was a monster, escaped from his box and angry.

"You planning on busting my windows?" he demanded.

The boys paused. This idea had never occurred to them.

"No," James said, because it was true.

Mel wasn't listening.

"I'm going to have to whup you, fat-face," Mel said to Reggie. He turned to James. "And you're not getting out of here either. When I'm done with fat-face I'm going to feed you his broken teeth."

Mel then looked at Willie and his forehead twitched. He said nothing, and again faced Reggie.

Mel held up his hands, not in fists, but as if displaying a fine set of knives. Reggie lifted his bat with both hands and seemed at once both bigger and smaller. James and Willie took unconscious steps away.

"I know what you did," growled Reggie.

"Yeah? What did I do?" asked Mel. "Hit too many home runs? Boy, that must've really pissed you off."

"We all know what you did," Reggie said.

James felt his head spinning; he felt warm, dizzy, hysterical.

"Mel didn't do anything," James cried, even though he couldn't remember if it was true. All he knew was that this fight was not about Willie Van Allen or Greg Johnson. Even worse, Mel's fight had nothing to do with Reggie, and Reggie's fight had nothing to do with Mel. They were just convenient targets set in front of two hitters dying to hit.

Neither James nor Willie knew exactly when the old man appeared on the porch behind Mel. He was frail, bent, and so pale he was nearly translucent. James and Willie saw him and blinked, their faces knotted in the sweltering sun. Despite the heat, the man wore flannel pajamas and a blanket was thrown over his shoulders. His yellowed hand curled around the handle of a cane. He also carted a strange blue object behind him from which snaked tiny plastic tubes that ran into what looked like an oxygen mask.

Reggie saw him next and instinctively lowered the bat. Mel did not turn around, but his large hands fell to his sides.

The old man licked his lips and gawked at the boys across the lawn. His skin was white and papery and there was a growth of beard on his face, irregular and lumpy like a fungus. There were hollows sunk into his neck. His feet were bare and his naked toes shrugged and gripped at the porch. His thin chest rose and fell, rose and fell. His pajama bottoms looked big enough for a man twice his size, and were speckled with paint in the same vivid colors as the house. This was not a man who could drive a truck or plot a killing; this was not a man who could bathe himself or reach the toilet without assistance.

They stood in the sun for a long time, the four boys and the old man. To James it was even worse than a fistfight. Somehow those old eyes upon him made him feel like he deserved whatever was coming: Mel's attack, his parents' punishments, a speeding silver truck, anything.

"My dad," blurted Mel. Blunt, hard, and coated with something–sickness? arrogance? satisfaction?–the two words shoved into James's ears and crashed around his skull, and continued to do so all the way home, past the motel, off Oleander Avenue, back through the trash-filled alley, across the Leisure Estates trailer park, over the train tracks, and then even further, for the entire rest of James's life, pounding forever through his veins like cold blood and lodging stiff and painful inside his heart.

Devil, Come Home Swiftly

The lathery stink of horsehide was suffocating, and the darkness made it worse. The space was narrow and the two boys bumped into the walls, each time causing a horse to snicker, flap its lips, stomp in place, grunt. The dust floated down like snow and the boys had to wipe it from their faces and necks and try to contain their sneezes, or else risk rousing the animals to some higher plateau of resentment.

The barn was hotter than anywhere else they had been that summer, maybe anywhere they had been in their lives. It was small and cramped, though it had looked enormous when they first approached it. There had to be a loft somewhere, but they saw no steps, no ladder, nothing. The building's sole feature was this single hall that ran one end to the other, bordered on both sides by horse stalls. The door to each stall was closed, but they were only half-doors and inside the boys could see the large, dark heads of the beasts outlined in moonlight.

James pressed his eyes into the floating dirt, searching for a sign of the Monster. They had discussed the Monster's location on the way over, and it had been Reggie who thought of the barn as the only sensible place.

"Tom wouldn't keep it outside," Reggie had said.

"Because people would steal it?" James asked.

"Because it's bones," Reggie replied. "And dogs and raccoons would come chew it up and drag it away."

So it was indoors, they agreed, but not in the house. Tom lived with parents and no parents they could conceive of would ever allow such a thing inside, certainly not in the same house where they ate their meals and took their baths and relaxed—all impossibilities with something like the Monster staring with its empty, meaningless eyeholes.

Therefore, the barn. It had to be in the barn. James had only nodded and kept moving, his heart racing, his palms sweating against the drawstrings of the empty laundry sack he carried. They would go into the barn, look for it, and maybe they would find it, maybe not. They would not encounter any people if they were lucky, and James clung to this single encouraging thought.

Neither of them had counted on the horses. Neither of them had foreseen creeping nearly shoulder to shoulder with these creatures, and in almost absolute darkness. Before his eyes had adjusted, James walked with one hand trailing against the wall for support, and suddenly the wall had dropped off and his hand had landed on something coarse and damp, and James had felt a quick, hot expulsion of air before pulling away, a scream gurgling in the back of his throat, for it was the Monster, *the Monster,* the Monster was *alive.*

Of course it had only been the nose of a horse, which really wasn't much better, and now James walked with his hands floating close at his sides, fearful of buckets left in the middle of the floor or pitchforks with unusually sharp points. He walked without raising his feet, instead shoveling them through the straw.

Reggie was somewhere up ahead, bothering the dust. He was in constant motion: on his knees, then on top of something, then poking his head into the abyss of a horse stall. These days James suspected more and more that Reggie found him useless and not much better than Willie.

James reached the end of the barn. Reggie's hands were fumbling their way across the wall.

"There has to be a loft," Reggie whispered. They both looked up, but the darkness withheld all details.

Reggie turned around and James did the same, and then they were looking back down the hall, where the walls were blacker than the floors, and the windows into each chamber blacker than even the walls.

"It's in with one of the horses," said Reggie, and his conviction was confirmation: they were going in, would move among each animal until they found what they were looking for, there was no way around it, it had to be done. James staggered. Surely they would be maimed. They would be knocked aside, their skulls crushed by powerful hooves.

Reggie moved forward. In despair, James spun his eyes wildly about the barn–what was he looking for? A weapon with which to intimidate Reggie? If James wanted to stop him, a weapon was what it would take, and he imagined tightening his fingers around the stem of a pitchfork, and how that single action would spell his end. Reggie, who seemed so much older now than at the start of the summer, would turn around and evaluate the feeble threat, and there might be a glimmer of regret in his eyes before he went at James with everything.

Then James's eyes found something he wasn't expecting and it was the Monster. He sputtered and attempted to speak as dust billowed into his mouth and dirt caked across his tongue. Reggie was reaching for a stall handle and James could not stop him and so he rabbit-thumped his sneaker against the ground.

It worked. Reggie turned to him and looked not so much older, after all, and James wagged a frantic finger. Above the door through which they had originally entered was a shelf, and on the shelf, propped among bags of feed, empty gas canisters, a coiled garden hose, and other assorted junk, was the Monster. Reggie saw it immediately and went for it.

By the time James got there, Reggie had already overturned a bucket, climbed on top, and taken hold of the apple box. It lifted quickly, as if Reggie had expected it to be heavier. Then he moved with confidence, hopping from the bucket and holding it out to James, grinning.

The gray of the bones glowed faintly. James did not want to move closer but he did until he could smell it, a weird mix of mud and manure and something else, something gamy. He felt all over again the confusion he felt the first time he saw the Monster. He knew he was supposed to experience awe—he had certainly felt it when hearing about it on the playground back in the spring— but now he fought for breath not out of admiration or fright but from an unexpected flood of revulsion. This thing in tatters and stuffed inside a box might be from a world of teenagers, grown-ups, and grandfathers, but it was foul and sickening and James wanted nothing of it.

Reggie took the laundry bag and kneeled down to shove the box inside. His rough movements made it clear: he did not care about the Monster, he never had, it was just a currency he could use to purchase entry into that life of cigarettes, cars, and girls. James realized that Reggie was just like Tom, for he too planned to exchange the Monster for something of greater value.

When they gently slid away from the barn, the laundry bag slung across Reggie's back, James was staggered by the expansiveness of the night; the sky seemed to retract and soar away. He stumbled and his head craned. Reggie put a hand against his back and shoved.

Their four hurried feet sounded like a stampede of horses.

Later, their walking was slow and soundless. James did not like it and asked Reggie what he planned to do with the Monster.

Reggie grinned and spun tales. What kid wouldn't hear about it, if not tomorrow, then the next day? And when school started up again, boy, the legend would spread like fire: there was a Monster and it was taken, and there was a boy who planned it and pulled it off— look, there he is.

But none of this answered James's question. What did he plan to *do* with it?

Reggie glanced at James in irritation, his smile fading. "What do you mean?" he asked. "I'll *have* it."

"But," James said, and then paused to consider his phrasing. It was as if Reggie could not see past this moment of flight. "But what do you want to *do* with it?"

"Well," said Reggie, looking at the sidewalk in front of him and automatically dodging the cracks. "I guess I'll put it away."

"Where?"

"I haven't decided yet. I guess in a box."

"Just like Tom's grandpa?"

Reggie did not look at him, but James felt the chill of his displeasure.

"I'll bring it out for special occasions," Reggie suggested. "I mean, that's what Tom said, right? It's special, it's the only thing like it anywhere. If I leave it out all the time, it won't be special at all, it won't even hardly be a monster. It'll just be something that, you know. That just sits there."

James gauged his advantage and spoke.

"Plus someone might steal it from you," he said. "I mean, if you leave it out."

Reggie kept his eyes on the task of skipping over cement cracks, but the temperature of his speech became cold like the earth when you dug too deep.

"Who's gonna steal it?"

"I don't know," said James. "I guess there's always somebody, though."

"Like who?"

James sighed like the whole thing was too confusing to think about, which was not true. He shrugged, and the shrug was exaggerated so Reggie would see it even in the dark, even as he studied the sidewalk.

"I don't know exactly," James said. "But how long did it stay up in that attic? A long time, right? And eventually someone stole it."

"Tom didn't steal it, it was his grandfather's, he took it from his dead grandfather."

"And then, after a while, we stole it from him," James said. "I'm just saying, there's always somebody. You can keep this thing locked up if you want, but one day you're going to have to take it out, or somebody's going to find it, or maybe you'll be dead and someone will just go through your attic. But eventually somebody's going to take it back."

Reggie was walking faster. He regripped the laundry bag.

"I'll bury it."

"All right," said James.

"No, I'll hide it in the junkyard. A special place in the junkyard, and we'll make a map, and draw up a map key that only makes sense to you and me."

"Someone could steal the key."

"Yeah, but you need both halves of the key to understand it, that's the thing."

"One of us could die, or move away, and then the other one would never be able find it, and then it's like we never even stole it, you know? Which is kind of even worse."

Reggie opened his mouth but caught his breath. Brushing accidentally against his arm, James felt how warm Reggie's skin was, even in the cool, late-night air.

They turned a corner and James's house was just ahead. Reggie suddenly swung the bag from his shoulders, tightened the string, and held it out to James.

"Hey" was all James could think to say.

"Here."

"What are you doing?"

"Take it."

"I don't want it."

Reggie smirked at him over the top of the bag. Brashness sharpened his features. James almost expected to see a cigarette dangling from his lip.

"I'm not giving it to you, dummy. But you know I can't take this inside my house."

James tried to stamp out the alarm that flared in his chest, but could not act fast enough.

"Why not?" He heard the whine in his voice but was unable to seal it off. "Why didn't you say something before? What do you expect me to do with it?"

Reggie made no sound, but it looked like he was laughing.

"Jesus, calm down. I'm not asking you to hang it in the living room. Just take it for tonight, stick it under your bed or something. Your house is huge, you got plenty of closets. If I show up with a bag like this my mom will see it right away, and then we'll both be in trouble."

It was a good threat. James still didn't know what to do and Reggie still held out the bag, and now they were only a few yards from James's driveway. Maybe if he sped up, if he scrambled up his lawn, maybe if he just did it fast enough, Reggie would have no choice but to deal with the bag himself.

"I'll come over tomorrow and get it from you. Once my mom leaves for work. It only makes sense. Come on, take it. It only makes sense. Aren't we in this thing together?"

With that, Reggie pressed the bag into James and

James took it and then Reggie smiled and nodded good-bye and broke away in the direction of his home, as if long aching to surpass James's drowsy pace. James stood at the foot of his driveway, grasping the bag in one elevated hand, alone.

Trying not to look at the bag, he walked slowly around to the back door. The bag smelled of nothing aside from dirty laundry; James held it an arm's length anyway. As he climbed the back stairs, the item inside the bag shifted. James shivered and goose bumps spilled from his sleeves, down his arms. He pressed open the squeaky door. The bag thunked against the doorframe. James grimaced and opened the door wider and suddenly the bag was inside, the Monster was inside his home, and the horror of it chased him to his bed, where he fell facedown into his pillow, wrapped clean sheets around his head, buried himself in a warm darkness, and then accidentally fell asleep.

* * *

His father held the bag by one hand. James could not yet react. It was not clear what time it was. James thought of what was inside the bag and then things went hot and awful and he felt like such a child, such a stupid, stupid child.

James and his father did not speak much anymore. The silence had begun the day James was caught lying about sleeping over at Reggie's. Now that James had seen his father with Call-Me-Kay at the run-down motel, he figured he knew how his dad had uncovered the truth. However, this suspicion remained unspoken and unproven—although he and his father lived in the same house and by necessity exchanged words, nothing but compulsory information passed between them. For the first time in his life, James heard nothing about the donut or the hole, and to his surprise he missed it. He ached to confront his father about Ms. Fielder so that things between them would return to normal, but before he could do that he felt he needed to gain his father's trust, become a man on equal footing.

That was a fantasy now. James had brought something illicit into the house, something dead, and that was breaking a law so basic it had never been formally stated. Did the cat drag in dead mice? Of course she didn't, and she was a dumb animal.

James felt a plummeting dread. How could he even begin to explain? His father would want to know what the thing was. James did not know. His father would want to know where it originated. James did not know. His father would want to know why he took it, why he wanted to bring it into their home. James felt like crying—he didn't know, he couldn't remember.

His father glanced at the bag in distaste and looked for a place to set it down. The floor was filled with boys' things—sneakers, army men, a baseball glove, a busted flashlight.

"You broke the curfew," said his father.

In his head, James begged for mercy.

His father looked away. "I'm not even angry about that. Boys do that. I get it. I'm not happy about it, but I get it, and it's a conversation for another day."

In fact, it was a conversation they'd had several times in the past—the rambunctious nature of boys, and how, if James was careful, it could safely extend all the way through college, no matter what James's mother said. All that was required was discretion, and James had failed even in that. He had brought an awful thing into their home, and this action not only jeopardized the future but also made his father vulnerable to his mother's rebuke.

James thought the time was right to speak. He chose his words, repeated them internally, and then tried them out: "I'm sorry."

His father seemed unmoved. His face was newly shaven, red and overly smooth, and the day was so young there was not yet a single pen poised inside his ink-stained pocket. His father's features pinched, and he rediscovered the bag in his hand. "I thought you had better judgment than this. Was your friend Reggie involved? He has an unkind influence on you, James, and I wish you could see that."

James felt his mind racing. He almost shouted, "Yes! Yes! It was Reggie!" but something in his gut raced even faster and stronger. He found himself shaking his head, protecting his friend, no, no, no—Reggie had nothing to do with this. Words even escaped his lips: "It wasn't Reggie."

His father raised his fist as if he were lifting a dumbbell, and looked at the lump that spun slowly from the draw straps.

"There's the stealing. That's one thing. I can't believe you'd do something like that, not without your friend Reggie, but who knows, maybe I'm wrong. Maybe I've misjudged you. Maybe you've disappointed me even more than I realize."

His father then did a terrible thing. He tossed the bag onto James's bed. James felt the weight of the apple box flop against his shin.

"I'll tell you what upsets me more," said his father, his voice rising. "That you believed in something this asinine. That we raised you–" He shut his mouth with a snap, looked for a moment as if he was doubting his words, then carried on in a tone less likely to wake James's mother. "That we raised you with certain values and certain goals, and still you behave in a way that could throw it all away. You have embarrassed me, James. You've really let me down."

This was the worst thing his father had ever said to him. James expected a flood of tears–they had certainly dropped from his eyes on lesser occasions–but for some reason the sobbing stayed caught in his chest. His nose felt full of snot. His hands were slimy with sweat. His neck was on fire.

"Take a look at it," his father said, jabbing his chin at the bag. "Go ahead, have a look. You went through a lot of trouble to get your Monster, you might as well see what it got you."

James dragged his eyes to the bag, and several moments passed before he realized what his father had said: he had called the Monster by its name. James looked at his father, so bewildered that he almost reached out. His father read his look and shrugged, and spoke to James slowly, like he was stupid.

"Of course I looked inside. And yes, I know what it is. Everyone knows what it is. Some kid out on Sycamore Lane with too much time on his hands. I tell you, it's this damn curfew, it's making you all stir-crazy." His father sucked on his teeth for a moment. "It's a prank, James. People make fun of it. It's some ridiculous old hoax. That kid? You should feel bad for him. He's not very smart, James. Not all kids are as smart as you. He's not very smart and you took advantage of him and you should feel bad."

James did feel bad, but not for those reasons. He looked at the bag, confused. What was it, then, that pressed its heavy weight against his shin?

Again his father read his mind and in an instant was leaning over the bed, opening the bag, and before James could scream or recoil, the apple box was yanked out and planted on the bed so hard the mattress shook. Particles of old, painted wood disintegrated into James's covers. A margin of dirt and dust marked where the box edges struck down against the sheets, and James knew he would never get the stain out, not ever.

His father pointed a finger at the Monster. "A pony skull. How can you not see that's a pony skull? And those bones there? What do you think they are? They're squirrel bones, tied together. You ever seen a dead squirrel on the road? These things here are called turkey feathers. James, those come from a turkey. Those—" Here he faltered, unable to immediately identify a delicate string of bones wired to one another. They looked to James like a human finger, and he thought of Willie's missing arm, how it had disappeared, how none of the boys knew what had become of it.

His father peered at the thing, momentarily fascinated before disgust once more overtook his features. "I'm just grateful no one will find out about this, because, James, if you think your little world is difficult now? You have no idea, you really don't. People would laugh and would hold it against you. Adults, teachers even. It's wrong, but that's what people do."

James said it again, only this time he didn't plan it, it just came out: "I'm sorry."

His father grabbed the apple box in one hand and hastily crammed it back into the bag. "Don't tell me," he said. "Tell that poor kid. We're taking this right back to where you got it. Come on, before your mother wakes up."

* * *

In fact it was still early morning, not even six. James did not know why his father was up so early—could it have been another odd-hour rendezvous with Reggie's mom? Even if that was true, James's numbness prevented him from producing a reaction. The two of them climbed into the family van and rode in silence, the laundry bag quivering on the floor between them.

He lifted a listless finger and pointed the way down the trail. When they arrived at Tom's house the morning was bright and clear. Tom was in the middle of the yard walking slowly toward them as they pulled to a stop, wiping his hands on his jeans and toeing aside a group of cats. Behind Tom, the barn doors were thrown wide on both ends, and in the field beyond the horses pondered the meager grass, their ribs visible even at a distance. The time had come for James to pick up the Monster and tell Tom what he had done.

James realized that this was the moment he had been waiting for, a way to prove he was a man worthy of his father's respect. But now that the moment was here he didn't want it. Stranger still, his father did not seem to want it either. There was regret in his dad's expression. His face softened and he looked down at James as if he were still a little boy in need of protection, and under such a gaze James felt exactly that way, fragile and helpless.

"We all have monsters," his father whispered. He reached over, picked up the laundry bag, stepped from the van, and began walking toward Tom. They met halfway across the yard.

James strained to watch without drawing attention to himself. He had to resist crying out in relief. He was off the hook! He wouldn't have to face Tom and meet those sad, crooked eyes. The pressure lifted and he breathed deeply, exhilarated, but then deeply repentant, too. As he watched his father's lips move, James swore to himself he would apologize when his dad returned to the van. He would make oaths about good behavior, he would ground himself, he would be a good boy for the rest of the summer—no, the rest of the year, all the way through Christmas. Reggie *was* a bad influence, clearly that was true, and James suddenly missed Willie Van Allen, an innocent kid who existed on a plane far removed from this one of guilt and shame. He would spend more time with Willie, work harder on his schoolwork, position himself to become the ideal college candidate, and this perpetual sickness he felt over disobeying his folks would finally dissipate. James felt optimistic, good about his father, about himself. Things would be all right. Things would be as they used to.

He watched his father hold out the bag and saw Tom raise both hands, palms out, before diverting his eyes and taking a step away, shrugging in disinterest. James's father held the bag a moment longer. Tom would not look at it—he stared out at the horses. Finally, James's father set the bag on the ground, said a parting word, and walked slowly back to the van.

His father slammed the door and started the engine. He looked tired and old, and occupied with matters too complicated for a little boy. James's promises, as earnest as they were, never reached his lips. The van wheeled around the yard. As they drove away, James hid his face and in the rearview mirror saw Tom look down at the laundry bag, which lay a motionless lump in the dirt. And right before a car filled with teenagers rumbled past, obscuring his senses with dust and smoke and music, James was pretty sure he saw Tom drop to one knee and smile.

An Animal Eats and Never Suffers Again

Reggie stood alone.

Seen up close, the baseball diamond was not as impressive as he had hoped. The bases were authentic, but flat and discolored. There was a mound but it was low and off-center, and if there was a pitcher's rubber it was lost beneath the dirt. There were no baselines at all; this realization was the harshest. He had imagined straight white lines of infinite distance, so sharply drawn not a single spot of powder broke rank.

Reggie hitched up the duffel bag on his shoulder. He moved with purposeful inelegance, scuffing his toes through the dirt and kicking up dry clouds, spitting and not watching where it landed. He slouched to home plate and threw down his bag with a thump, and did not look to see where the bats rolled, how many balls escaped and lost themselves in the backstop weeds. He coughed—an unnecessary sound that announced his presence as well as his disregard for those who might hear it—and wiped his palms across his shirt. He felt the heat of his armpits dampen the wispy hair that grew there.

He grabbed a bat and weighed it in his arms. He experimented with a few half-swings, not knowing what he was looking for but nevertheless enjoying the search, and then tossed it aside and picked up another. Yes, this one would do.

He palmed a ball and tossed it into the air and immediately lost it in the sunset glare. But he was a boy, he'd done this a million times before, and though blind he swung with assurance and felt the satisfying jolt of bat striking ball, and heard the distant thuds of it skipping across the infield and whisking through outfield grass.

His ears, trained on the junkball diamond, calculated the thuds. This field was larger. Good, it should be. For five years, from a distance, he'd watched the impossibly tall and impossibly talented high school boys play here on weeknights and weekends—sometimes even during regular school hours, which amazed Reggie to no end— the offhand poise of their every catch and throw somehow more startling than that of the televised pros.

Today the field was vacant. Too hot, Reggie figured,

sweat sliding down his eyelids. No matter, he was here to play. Maybe the teenagers would show up later, in twos and threes, smoking and laughing and hanging all over each other, and then they'd discover him, some twelve-year-old kid who played like he was born in a dugout.

Reggie turned around and reached into his bag for another ball. He found none and looked to the backdrop weeds, yet resisted getting on his knees to search for the balls surely hiding within. Instead he pulled his cap farther down on his head, and charged across the field, bat in hand. He'd find the ball he just hit, and smack it back across the field. The simplicity of the idea appealed to him.

Why not? The summer was dying like a cigarette. Reggie could almost feel the months wear away like an arm or leg waking from a deep sleep, and the resulting tingling sensation drew his attention to his own body: baked brown, strong and quick. He would play here all night if he felt like it. Who could stop him? He felt invincible and instantly knew it to be the truth. He was.

He found the ball, picked it up, tossed it into the air, hit it. It rang against the batter's-box chain-link. Before the ball even came to rest Reggie was charging at it, faster this time, grabbing for it, tossing it up again, feeling muscles clench across his back, a textbook swing. He went after it. He felt himself wear down to a series of meaningless repetitions, and it felt exciting and adult because he could perfect these repetitions if he wanted.

There was nothing better to do. His grandest scheme

had been ruined when James had lost the Monster. Even though Reggie had felt a peculiar sort of relief when he had found out, he still manufactured some resentment toward James, who had made the classic child's mistake of falling asleep too quickly.

And then there was Willie, who a few days ago found his way to the junkball field and made a scene in front of James and the other players. He yelled at Reggie for not inviting him along to steal the Monster. He made other weepy accusations about flashlight beams in his tree house, about being left behind for junkball, about being left behind, period. Reggie did not feel anger toward Willie as he led him aside and nodded for the other boys to go ahead, keep playing, this wasn't going to take very long. Willie was wild-eyed, one-armed, his cheeks red, his balance precarious. Reggie said very little and tried to scoot Willie along his way. He actually pushed him in the direction of home, firmly but gently, feeling the twiggy fragility of Willie's backbone beneath his shirt.

Then James came to Willie's aid and things complicated. Reggie had been expecting something like this from James for days. Following their failure with the Monster, James had shunned anything even remotely connected with fun, always went home before curfew, and talked about the upcoming school term like it was something he anticipated. Even getting James to the junkyard had been a struggle.

Suspicions were now confirmed: James was on Willie's side. There was silence from the boys as Reggie examined his feelings. It did not take long, as he found very few feelings at all. He told James to mind his own business and then there was shouting—Reggie could no longer remember specifics—about how you don't abandon friends, treat them like garbage, stuff like that. It gave him a headache.

So Reggie chose a remark that would shut James up: "When I saw your dad at my house, he didn't mention anything about the Monster—if that's what's got you so uptight." Reggie felt some regret speaking aloud these facts, though he was not sure why. He knew facts could not hurt you, not if you chose to ignore them. James, though, looked angry and confused all at once, and as a result could not act upon either emotion. James instantly faded back; Reggie felt serene; and then Willie came to James's defense, roaring, spoiling everything.

Nearly foaming, Willie leapt forward and hit Reggie, a girlish knock of knuckles against Reggie's chest—nothing, really—but before Reggie could retaliate, Willie's fist was back, this time against his chin, then nose, then throat, and though none of the blows was key, together they worked: Reggie was backpedaling, his arms were rising to shield his face. He felt Willie's forehead thump into his ribs, felt hot spit tack across his cheek, felt fingernails rake down his side, and none of it made sense, this was not how boys fought. There was no method at all to Willie's attack, if that was what it was, and Reggie gasped at the heat now rushing up his neck—why, he was *scared*. This feeling quickly turned into anger, for it reminded

Reggie of a year ago, when he still cried over minor injuries, still felt sorry for himself that no one kissed his boo-boos. He was not that boy anymore—he knew it, he just had to remember it.

He banked to the side, lifting his shoulder to protect himself, and felt Willie's entire weight smash into his back; there was a wheeze from Willie and a surprised bleat from James. Willie's arm wrapped around Reggie's knees and he felt Willie's arm-nub wedge inadvertently into his groin. More in disgust than anything else, Reggie made an instinctive hop to the right, and moments later both boys rolled their bodies through the dirt. Reggie, having two arms, was the first back on his feet.

Willie hurled his arm at Reggie but the blow seemed to take forever; Reggie even had time to see the blood-brother scar that marked the center of Willie's palm. Reggie made use of the moment. All right, there it was, easy—he saw just how to prevail. Reggie stepped to the right and struck Willie once in the chest. Willie coughed and to his credit immediately swung at Reggie again, but again Reggie shifted right and struck Willie's chest, knocking him back. James made jerky movements in the background, like he was dying to get in there and feel the collision of bone yet for some reason could not do it. Willie snorted and hacked but kept coming, his knotted face now as disfigured as his body, but Reggie kept moving away from Willie's remaining arm: to the right, right, right.

After too many circulations spent swatting at the air,

Willie at last landed choking and crying in the dirt. In front of all the other junkball players, it was utter humiliation: snot, tears, slobber, all cascading down his face and neck. Much too late, James found a small amount of courage and moved to Willie's side. He lifted him, slinging an arm around his heaving body and pressing his cheek into the burning wetness of Willie's own. Bound together, they limped away. Hours later, when Reggie himself left the junkball field, he knew something none of the other boys knew. He was never coming back.

Reggie's shirt was now a second skin, slopped to his torso with a bucket of sweat. He peeled it off with a snap and tossed it in the dirt. He hit the ball, ran after it. Hit the ball, ran after it. This was no longer junkball he was playing, this was baseball. No—it wasn't baseball either, but something more, some military ordeal he could not bring himself to quit. He was not sure why. He felt his head spin. His lungs ached with each guzzle of air. His muscles trembled and threatened to collapse. It was torture, but inevitable and necessary, like rings through ears, ink into skin, the swallowing and heaving up of alcohol.

His eyes stopped seeing. There remained a blur of dim light, but he operated now on his other senses, the smell of sweat, the troubled hiss of dead grass, the rotten texture of the tape wrapped around the bat. The narrower Reggie's focus, the more confident he became in his strength and cunning. Brains did not mean memorizing lists of figures like James, or stupid strings of words like Willie. Brains were figuring out how to swipe the answer key from the teacher's desk. Brains were figuring out how to ingratiate yourself with bigger and more powerful people, until *you* were the one big and powerful. That was what he was doing on this field, this field upon which no other kid his age dared tread.

The rush of superiority was strange and wonderful. For so long he had felt that his abilities lagged behind those of James and Willie. He had met James in third grade, and the first thing he'd appreciated about him was his ability to take a punch. That's right—he remembered it now. At recess, just beyond the monkey bars, where a group of older kids had held James in a headlock while his face grew purple. When James had finally dislodged himself there had been a flurry of blows and James had come away bloody. It was an expected series of events with expected results—the nurse's office, an ice pack, the works—but instead James turned away, snorting the blood into his throat and spitting it out in forceful globs. Reggie tracked him at a distance, admiring each red splotch as they grew smaller and diminished into the blacktop. Reggie made contact with James that afternoon, and by nightfall they were friends.

Reggie had known Willie even longer, since kindergarten. Back then they had been the same size, and remained that way for years. He remembered being on his knees in a playground sandbox, and how Willie had shown him how to construct fantastic underground labyrinths. He had loved Willie for that, and had continued to love him for the inventions he created in first grade (melted-chocolate tar pits for their plastic dinosaurs), second grade (faked UFO photographs using cardboard cutouts and clean windows), and so on.

But as years passed, Reggie spent too many recesses indoors redoing botched homework, and would locate James and Willie through the classroom window and feel twinges of resentment. *What am I doing wrong?* he used to think. Now he knew he had done nothing wrong. Because here he was, stronger, smarter, and fiercer than his two former playmates, and any remaining jealousy now turned into something closer to pity.

Willie's body had stagnated while Reggie's had grown thicker and taller. Willie's teeth had spread like petals on water, while Reggie's baby teeth twisted out with force and blood, and replaced themselves with teeth stronger and larger. It now seemed to Reggie that Willie had lost an arm because it ceased to have any worth—it could not help Willie, so it withered away and died. Even Willie's mind had lost its way, trapping itself within a loop of senseless wordplay. Reggie thought it would be sad when Willie finally realized all of the living that he had missed.

James's transformations had been less dramatic, but Reggie's sharp eye noticed them all: his anxiety, his timidity, his obsession with a future already plotted out by his parents. Though physically James was not unlike Reggie, he could not make a move without tripping over one thought and blundering into another. Reggie felt again the finely burning point of his own focus and was thrilled.

There were so many things he could no longer tell James and Willie: the blunt words of high school boys, the laughter and occasional touches of teenage girls, the satisfaction of a thick roll of paper money in his back pocket rather than the delicate jingle of pennies and nickels and dimes.

Most of all Reggie could not tell James and Willie what he knew about Mel Herman. Weeks ago, Reggie had snuck back inside the school. He'd told no one, because he was no longer interested in their admiration. This time he had waited until just after sundown, then experimented with first-floor windows until one of them slid open. Once he was inside, the familiar isolating chill had gripped him, but he plunged through the darkness, telling himself it was like dunking your head underwater for the first time. Surely he'd resurface alive.

When he left the school a short while later, he had his flashlight stuffed in one pocket of his shorts and the rest of Mel Herman's handiwork rolled up and jammed under his arm. Instead of walking home, Reggie made a detour and climbed into Willie's tree house, and sat cross-legged inside it, alone. He turned on his flashlight and examined all of the paintings. He found objects that might have been Mel's house, contorted shapes that could have been Mel's father. James was better at this kind of stuff—the more Reggie studied, the less certain he became of anything.

He returned again to the first painting they'd stolen and aimed his flashlight beam at the detail that had started everything: a tiny truck running over a tiny person. At the beginning of the summer, it had been as good as a confession of guilt, but now Reggie looked closer and found something altogether different. It wasn't a truck, or a car, or anything. It was a bunch of lines. That person caught beneath the wheels—that wasn't a person and those weren't wheels. He wondered how the three of them had rushed to the same mistake.

So Reggie had done something else that night, something James and Willie would have called absolute madness. He climbed from the tree house with all of Mel Herman's paintings—aside from the original one, which he left tacked to the tree house wall—and walked all the way to Mel's home. For a while he stood in the shadows. From inside he heard music playing from a radio and bathwater running. Then he heard arguing: the old man's gravelly voice and Mel's rare, tentative responses. Reggie carefully placed Mel's paintings next to the front door, weighted them down with a rock, and then went home.

Two days later there was a Mel Herman painting, a brand-new one, sitting on Reggie's doorstep. Reggie looked at it for a while. It did not make sense. Or did it? Could that diamond be the junkball field? Could that straight line be the baseball bat that he had threatened Mel with outside his house? It really didn't matter, for the painting was large and brilliant blue and wonderfully menacing; Reggie *wanted* to understand what it meant and somehow wanting to understand was good enough.

Reggie taped it to his bedroom wall and it became even more obvious. The color was just color, the paint just paint. Mel Herman was simply a kid who placed paint wherever he pleased. The significance of this was breathtaking; suddenly Mel was no longer a foe. He pictured Mel slouching through the halls two weeks from now when school resumed, and imagined how they might speak to each other and what they might say. Finally he fantasized about all the new things Mel might show him, for there was only one thing Reggie was sure of when it came to Mel Herman. He was *bigger*.

The air was heavy and itchy. He tossed the ball, swung the bat, chased after. Hit, run. Hit, run. Reggie's knees pumped up and down and sweat dripped from his nose. He tried to catch his breath and could not, and found he did not care. He kept moving, faster, wondering with morbid fascination when exactly his body would collapse. Hit, run, hit, run.

The world darkened. Caught within the curfew's grip, the daylight hours all summer had felt curtailed and constricted. But who needed daytime? The night unrolled itself and expanded before Reggie's sightless eyes into something he could explore forever, live inside. He drank air like dark water and grew accustomed to it, found oxygen, decided he liked it, no, loved it.

The moon rose and the curfew descended. To hell with it. Let them come: teenagers, grown-ups, killers, police waving flashlights and nightsticks. If they came and took him away he'd be even stronger, because then he'd be one of them. Reggie closed his eyes, blind now for good, and felt the veins of the baseball press into his equally leathery palm, the heavy bat lift from his even heavier shoulder, and he pushed himself harder. Hit, run, hit, run, hit, run.

Every Good Boy Deserves Forgiveness

"How do you see so much?" demands Miss Bosch from her bed.

Mel Herman shrugs. "I just keep my stupid eyes open."

Mel tells Miss Bosch about the violence he sees and hears about all over town. She responds that it is an odd thing that the summer ended up so bloody. Spring is the season of birth, she says, and that's a naturally violent thing; autumn is the season of slaughter and death. Not this year, says Mel.

Every day he tries to find something to tell her, either

overheard from one of his odd-job employers or memorized from the police blotter, lately his favorite section of the local paper—which he reads now instead of throws. Mel Herman tells these things to Miss Bosch because he likes her wicked smiles and thirsty, mean-spirited cackles.

These are the things Mel Herman tells her: In late July, four kids make a pipe bomb in a backyard and it blows up while still in some kid's lap, and he loses four fingers and the hair from the top of his head. For weeks afterward, kids marvel at the resulting stain and wonder to one another why no one has bothered to clean it.

A grown-up shoots a hole through his own hand with a hunting rifle. A teenager hooks his eyebrow with a fishing lure while out on Grayson Lake. A curious little girl sticks her tongue inside a metal soda can and the can must be cut away by surgeons. A woman falls down in the local movie theater and on the dark, sticky floor there is blood but no one can see where it comes from. A head wound? Busted lip? Or maybe from somewhere inside? And everything in between is worse this year, too—Mel can attest to it. Skinned knees are skinned wider, bloody noses gush harder, cuts are deeper, scrapes nastier, puncture wounds so severe that it takes almost a minute for the blood to well and push its way out from the hole.

"They don't trust anyone who doesn't bleed suitably," says Miss Bosch, barely audible beneath the clanging of that rusty old fan. Mel thinks she is referring to herself, dying slowly but with nothing at all to prove it:

no wounds, no blood, no plastic tubes in her nose like his father. Each day Mel spends more and more time at Miss Bosch's bedside, scrutinizing her rising and falling torso and wondering if each breath he witnesses is her last.

"Paint for me," she says one day.

She knows about his painting. He doesn't remember how, but somehow over the summer she has dragged the information from him. He says no. No, thank you. But the request sets fire to his insides. No one has made such a request from him since his brother asked him to paint all those album covers.

Anyway, Mel knows Miss Bosch doesn't really want him to paint for her, she's just being polite. Once she saw his work, Mel is certain that she would ignore it like his brother, or misunderstand it like Mr. "Bud" Camper. No, thank you, ma'am.

Mel doesn't know what to do about Mr. Camper, who one blistering day around lunchtime catches Mel slouching down the street. Mr. Camper tells him he has been calling Mel's home for days but no one answers, and when Mr. Camper drove to Mel's house last Friday, no one came to the door. Mr. Camper, beneath his unkempt beard and long hair and ruffled clothing, is excited. There's an arts academy in the city, he says. A scholarship you're being offered, he says. He has pamphlets and information and he tries to show them to Mel right there in the middle of the road. Mel's heart beats so hard that the veins in his throat squeeze off his air. He takes the pamphlets from Mr. Camper without looking at them and hurries away, feeling cold sweat trickle down the middle of his back. Mr. Camper hollers that Mel must call him, and soon, because the academy's application deadline is just ten days away—there isn't much time! Mel mumbles, thank you Mr. Camper, and Mr. Camper hollers back, please, Mel, call me Bud.

Mel goes home and tosses the paperwork in the garbage.

Later that week, when Mel returns home from his daily roaming with a handful of money collected from Miss Bosch, Mr. and Mrs. Huron, Ms. Daisy, Mr. Coleman, and several others, his father is waiting for him in the living room, clutching paper in a skeleton fist. Mel is frozen. There in his father's hand are the pamphlets and application forms from Mr. Camper, only wrinkled and dappled with tomato sauce, coffee grounds, and bacon grease. His father shakes the papers; some of them flutter to the floor. His father is upset. He's always upset, but this time it is different. He screams so loudly saliva swings from his chin. Mel stands there like a boxer taking punches.

His father yells for hours, and afterward Mel still is not sure why. His father does not say he wants Mel to put the papers back in the trash. His father also does not say he wants Mel to go to a special arts academy in the city. He only rattles his blue oxygen tank and roars about being left alone to die. Hacking and spluttering and coughing, tears of incredulity leaking from his red eyes, Mel's father demands his bath. Mel disconnects the oxygen tank and helps his father move slowly to the tub, then removes his father's clothes and lifts him into the lukewarm water.

His father seems to weigh less than the weapon that presses against Mel's chest.

With his father splashing safely in the tub, Mel goes to his bedroom and shuts the door. He peels off his filthy black shirt. Then, as he does every night, he gingerly removes the object that he has carried next to his heart all summer: his brother's knife, what the high schoolers call a switchblade, and he unfolds it and watches how the dull light from the ceiling's bulb transforms into white shimmers when it strikes the clean, sharp blade.

When his father calls to be removed from the tub, Mel clenches his weapon. The knife is a way out, he knows this, a better way out than any worthless arts academy, any meaningless scholarship.

Now the phone rings almost every night. Mel answered it the first time, but it was Mr. Camper, and Mel hung up without saying a word.

"You have no business taking a scholarship," says Miss Bosch when she hears of it. Mel didn't mean to tell her about Mr. Camper's offer, but somehow it just came out. "Isn't that right?" she asks. Mel shrugs. Miss Bosch looks thinner and weaker than ever. She is dying, as sure as Mel's father is dying, but instead of flailing like a drowning man she is sinking straight down like a brick.

Miss Bosch laughs, a raspy, crackling chuckle. "No

academy would ever want someone like you," she says. "Isn't that right?"

She then demands that he paint for her, as she does now every day. But Mel has made a decision: no more painting, not ever. If he just stops that foolishness, right here, right now, the distress it causes in everyone—his father, Miss Bosch, Mr. Camper, himself—will go away.

One evening as he fixes his father's bedtime poached eggs and toast, the newly coined cusswords of "scholarship" and "academy" still sputtering from his father's lips, Mel hears a sound from the doorstep. Mel leaves the stove and peeks from behind the curtain, afraid that he will see Mr. Camper.

Instead, he sees a kid from school named Reggie Fielder, and a pile of school paintings stacked beneath a heavy rock. Instantly he remembers Reggie standing outside his garage a couple weeks ago, with that kid James Wahl and that one-armed Willie Van Allen, and the way Reggie held that baseball bat like he was going to start swinging. Mel doesn't even think about it: he grabs his brother's switchblade and his heart leaves his body, he is capable of anything. He is at the door, the knife is brandished. He is breathless.

But the weight of the weapon drags down his hand. Reggie Fielder leaves. When Mel goes out later to inspect Reggie's delivery more closely, the rock looks like a grave marker. Beneath the marker, Mel's paintings are dead.

Later that night, a resurrection: Mel Herman decides to make one final painting.

Reggie's house is even smaller than Mel's. The new painting, his final one, Mel leaves at Reggie's doorstep, killed dead beneath another rock. Even Mel is not sure what the painting is supposed to say to Reggie. It could be a warning. It could also be an invitation. Mel has a strange urge not to terrorize Reggie with his knife, but to show him the blade, show him how the spring-release works.

"Paint for me," demands Miss Bosch a few hours later. Her voice is a thin piece of paper, perhaps an application to an arts academy, fluttering away too fast in the wind.

Mel remembers Miss Bosch complaining that the townspeople "don't trust anyone who doesn't bleed suitably." Maybe Miss Bosch had not been talking about herself after all. Maybe she had been speaking about Greg Johnson or Willie Van Allen. Clean crime scenes are suspicious—where is the blood, aside from reproduced somewhere in one of Mel's paintings? Death, Mel thinks, is the most suspicious thing of all, for once the bodies are gone, how can you be sure they ever existed? Mel's brother is gone but that does not necessarily mean he is dead; so a marble marker reading "Gregory Johnson" does not, in fact, prove anything.

As he continues his odd jobs, Mel finds further evidence that he is right: he can sense the dawning disbelief in the hit-and-run killer in everything the grown-ups say and do. There is blood all around them, yes—that they can plainly see. But a murder? When? Says who? A murder without a victim or assailant is not a murder, it is daily life.

"Chew your food," Mr. and Mrs. Huron warn their children. Mel smoothes down the new dining room linoleum and watches the bored, too-safe Huron family grind their jaws until their food is a flavorless mash impossible to choke on. Mel has seen these children so bored at night that they touch stove burners and fondle broken glass, practically dying for danger. Mel watches the children drag their feet inside at eight o'clock. Television schedules are fought over. Board games are dusted off. Tiny plastic playing pieces go missing and paper money is doled out. A banker is elected. Free Parking rules are irritably debated. None of the Hurons is happy.

"This curfew," sighs Ms. Daisy into her phone as Mel mops up another kitchen flood. She sips her tea and chats to someone on the other end about the Van Allens, who continue to have a rough time, or at least that's the current gossip. Mr. Van Allen has been out of work now for what seems like forever, and Mrs. Van Allen has been seen laughing too loudly in the cereal aisle and standing in front of playgrounds, crying into her hand. "This is the bed we've made ourselves," Ms. Daisy whispers into the phone as Mel slips out the back door to dump the foul water.

"Sleep tight," says Mr. Coleman, checking on his tucked-in kids. Mel stands quietly, awaiting payment and listening to Mr. Coleman chew the ice from his second or third stiff drink. Mr. Coleman clears his throat and speaks about being a child himself, about his own childhood injuries and accidents, as well as some things that were not accidents at all. "Being a kid has never been a very safe thing," Mr. Coleman tells Mel with a shrug.

All of this means less to Mel Herman now that his painting has ceased. He still hears everything but no longer has any reason to remember it. "Doing nothing is death, too," snaps Miss Bosch, straining her dry eyes through the arid current of the metal fan. Mel feels the weight of his switchblade and wonders if using it on Miss Bosch would be merciful or cruel. "Doing nothing, Mel Herman, is a more gradual death than that by truck," Miss Bosch continues from where she lies, sunk deep down in her bed. "But every parent has warned their child against standing still in the middle of the road. You know why?"

Miss Bosch smiles that wicked smile.

"If you want to live, you've got to *move*."

A Common, Everyday Grave

The curfew: lifted!

All across town the news was delivered by parents glancing over the tops of newspapers. Some grown-ups relayed the news with skepticism; these were the parents who felt that no child had business scurrying around after nightfall anyway. Other grown-ups spoke from a sideways smile hidden behind the sports section; these were the parents who remembered the headlong thrill of charging, too fast, over a field turned purple with night. Some grown-ups reacted in ways that none other could predict, like Mrs. Van Allen, who clapped her hands ferociously, as if this marked the beginning of some new and better phase, while Mr. Van Allen sat shivering at the kitchen table, his hands in fists, perhaps cursing the killer, that son of a bitch, who was going to get away after all. Still other grown-ups, like Reggie's mother, did not even hear the news; she awoke late, as usual, and messed her son's hair on her way out the door. Reggie smoothed down his hair without thinking about it—the curfew was lifted!

The kids understood the math. It had been almost three months since the hit-and-run driver killed Greg Johnson. It had been even longer since Willie Van Allen lost his arm. Apparently the grown-ups had decided that these two incidents were unrelated—basically just rotten luck—and that if there was a real killer, he had long ago left town.

So at the last moment, just one week from the start of classes, summer returned to them, less dangerous than before and therefore less desirable. Some boys stood in circles and kicked the dirt, like they did at the beginning-of-summer fair, and some wondered why they had become blood brothers at all, if not to defy curfews. When Friday night faded into Saturday morning, boys all across town opened their eyes to a world without danger, and it felt to them like a body drained of blood.

They felt safe.

* * *

Long vampire claws lashed at their cheeks. No, they were tree branches, trying to hold them back. But they could not stop, would not stop—once more they were running too fast.

Tonight Reggie ran first but only because there was no time at all for getting lost. He pushed through thorn bushes, hurdled fallen maples, barreled through nets of underbrush. Directly behind him was Willie, who kept his eyes trained on the moon glow of Reggie's white T-shirt, suffering visions of dropped eggs and discarded milk, but determined to never again fall behind. Lagging several yards back was James, for some reason having more trouble with the trees and weeds and sticks and stones. Of course, part of this was Willie's fault—he kept letting branches whip back into James's face.

A woman was screaming. No, it was the wind.

It was horrible, what they had heard—and just one day after the curfew had been dropped? It was too much to be mere coincidence. James had heard it first, through his bedroom floor, as his mother gasped into the telephone. His father was absent, working late yet again, but his mother provided James plenty to chew on. After she hung up, she told Louise the whole thing, then dialed one friend, then another, and in this fashion the news, as well as the speculation on who would do such a ghastly thing, vibrated out through telephone wires to grown-ups all over town as well as to their eavesdropping children. James remained crouched on his floor, hardly breathing. Of course he knew that Reggie and Willie would want to know—they'd *need* to know—only he was afraid to tell them. Because if he told, Reggie would want to see it.

Then there were footsteps on the roof and Reggie was there, his ghost face at the windowpane, just like old times. Out of habit, James let him in. Reggie's expression made it clear that the news had already reached him. There passed a moment when one of them could have laughed or smiled or done something to stamp out the dread. But that moment left them and their silent faces made it worse. It was Reggie Fielder and James Wahl—once the best of friends—and neither could utter a word.

They were out the window and down the side of the house, away. Together they threw stones at Willie's window and hid shoulder to shoulder beneath the tree house. They waited. Five minutes, ten minutes. The night deepened. The hot wind ruffled their hair warmly, as if they stood abreast a bonfire.

As they waited, James stole glances at Reggie. As far as James was concerned, the fight on the junkball field was not finished. He could not forgive himself for failing to come to Willie's aid, for being so afraid, and so still he waited to take the next blow. But even this, James knew, would be overlooked tonight.

Then Willie ran out the door—ran!—and it was instantly clear that the Van Allens had heard, too, because they could hear from inside the snatches of rage and bafflement: "—never should've lifted the curfew, I *told* them"; "Barry, why are they doing this to *us*?" Willie's braces glimmered from his open mouth and his eyes were shining. The boys stood looking at one another for a moment—again, if only one of them had said something the spell might've been broken and then maybe one of them would've been brave enough to say, "No, this is crazy, we don't need to see it," and the other two might've agreed—but then, from inside, they heard more wailing and the chain rattle of car keys, and that was all it took. They were running again, their skin erupting in goose bumps even though the evening was sticky.

Naturally every boy in town would want to see this, but Reggie alone claimed knowledge of a secret back route that avoided all lit roads. So they dove into the timber. Now, hurtling through the trees, the time for worrying was past. They would be there shortly, and then the truth would separate itself from rumor.

James kept his legs turning and did not know how he continued to find footholds on the black, uneven terrain. It felt as though he was fleeing something fearsome and gaining—maybe it was a silver truck, maybe it was Willie's parents, or maybe he was simply trying to outrun the summer, which had finally come home, fattened and vengeful. School began soon, he knew that, and all things, even summers, eventually died. But perhaps if you ran fast enough, you'd never have to witness the actual moment of passage.

It hit all three boys at once, the terrible possibility that they were lost. They had never played in these woods before. They certainly hadn't expected to cross that creek. Were they wildly off course, heading now into the deeper, darker jaws of something waiting to swallow them? There was no telling what creatures prowled in such woods: bobcats, bears, wolves, spiders, snakes, maybe even other boys who had lost themselves in the forest years before.

James knew it was hopeless—they should've come out the other end of these trees long ago. Willie glanced back at him and James recognized the same fear, but Willie's expression warned James to keep quiet. James weighed the moment. If he spoke his dissension aloud, his voice might become his own missing arm.

Then Reggie slowed. The other two pressed up behind. There, before them, was a fence. It was wrought iron and tall. They had arrived. They looked beyond the fence and their shoulders shuddered and their guts hardened.

Gravestones spread across the cemetery at regular intervals like the protruding vertebrae of a buried monster a thousand times larger than Tom's. It was a calculated risk: if the boys dared trespass, might not the Monster rise and reveal the rest of its hideous skeleton?

The boys had cleared bigger fences in their day.

They helped Willie vault over the top—the maneuver was the same used to hoist him up to Mel Herman's garage. Once alone on the other side, Willie looked back through the bars. James shivered. It was like seeing Willie on the other side of the Van Allens' screen door, only this time his home was a cemetery—*this was where he lived.* Perhaps he was supposed to have died when the truck hit him, and the cemetery just wanted him back.

Seconds later Reggie was over the fence. Burying his

dread, James followed suit and then they stood together at the far perimeter of the graveyard, three boys versus a legion of the dead, and they advanced without weapons because of the one desire that conquered even terror: the desire to see.

They moved silently through the stones. They kept expecting to see it, to see *something*–a gathering of grown-ups, other curious children, maybe even newspaper reporters. When they finally saw it in the distance, they realized they had been looking at it for some time. There were no crowds. There were no lights. There was only the glisten of police tape tied from tree to tree.

The boys slowed but kept walking. Soon they could read the yellow tape: POLICE LINE DO NOT CROSS. Then they were at the tape, then they ducked beneath it, and then they held their breath as they looked upon it. The rumor was true.

Greg Johnson's grave was a tilled mash of dirt and grass. The headstone had been knocked back and now jutted at an angle. They could see the words GREGORY JOH but a great chunk of stone had gone missing and with it the rest of the name. The boys stepped closer and allowed their feet, through their thin sneaker soles, to feel the soft mounds of dirt vomited up from Greg's grave.

A truck had done this. Someone had driven his truck harmlessly through the entire cemetery and then ripped his tires into Greg's burial plot, yanking his vehicle violently back and forth, breaking Greg's headstone and accelerating so that the truck wheels spun in place and sliced deep furrows into the ground.

Although there was no blood, it looked to the boys like carnage. Both Reggie and James remembered how the area had looked at Greg's funeral, the lines of the plot drawn so neatly within the cemetery's geometric grid. Was the culprit a high school hooligan out for a sick giggle? Was it the work of a surly grown-up hoping for the resumption of the curfew? Or was it, as everyone had been whispering all evening, a taunting reminder that the hit-and-run killer was still among them?

Willie ventured the closest, climbing right on top of the soft mound of earth. He kneeled down, dirtying his knees, and grabbed a handful. Suddenly all the things they had done that summer—good things, bad things, awful things—ran off the edges of their minds like dirt spilling through five little fingers.

A grinding noise. A low growl.

Wheels.

Engine.

A truck.

They heard it together and they collectively heaved, each boy in a different direction, and they each darted a few feet before realizing they were alone, and then they ran at each other and collided like fools, legs tangling, fingers poking eyes. Reggie ended up on the ground; James pressed a palm to his scratched cheek; Willie was several feet away, blinking his eyes, dazed.

Silence. Nothing. They were okay. Everything was fine—

Then: *Whoonnnk!* A horn, and the splattery growl of an engine. And suddenly the boys ran, diving through the arms of seizing shadows, lacing in and out of headstones. They were not heading to the fence and the forest, no, this time they were sprinting toward the cemetery's front gate, the quickest way out.

From somewhere, everywhere, the truck, louder.

They didn't have time to locate it. Was it on a nearby road? Was it coming from deeper inside the cemetery, where the driver had idled in darkness, awaiting the perfect moment to strike? The boys kept running.

There was the front gate! Of course the grown-ups had locked it, double-chained it, but the boys paid it no mind. They ran harder, the engine noise now filling their heads and sinuses, until it seemed that the truck was directly on top of them and any second now they would feel the bone crack of the grill punching into their backs.

The fence: they executed formation, feet into palms, hands grasping wrists, legs flung—and they were over it. Six feet banged down on the other side, then kept running, down the driveway to the street and up the center of the street toward home.

It was a ghost town—or maybe the boys were just running too fast to see anyone. All they knew were the paved roads beneath them, jarred and vibrating with each brutal landing of shoes. Somewhere above, a sky and a moon. And somewhere behind them . . .

The truck?

A moment's hesitation—maybe it was just the roll of summer thunder, not an engine, and maybe those bobbing headlights behind them were just porch lamps flickering with moths. No, it had to be a truck, somehow escaped from the cemetery confines and now gunning its engine in another crazed attempt to catch them.

In their panic, single words expelled within jets of gasped air.

". . . Willie's house . . ."

". . . go to Willie's . . ."

Willie's house was the closest, and the only possible haven. They knew that grown-ups could not help and would not believe. A grown-up would say there was no truck, and maybe they would be right. This possibility was the worst of all—that the grown-ups were right and had been right all along, and that there was nothing following them, nothing to fear, and no reason at all to run. So they kept running.

And there at the dead end of the street was the Van Allen house. They felt their faces stretch with thankful grins, and they began to slow. But then it was right there around the bend, the metallic cry of a truck—a different one, the same? Who knew, and who had time to find out? The boys made fists and faces and tossed their chests into the wind and ran. Willie, somehow, kept up and did not lose balance.

They veered off the road, across the Van Allen lawn, past the doorway. They knew where they were heading without pausing to gasp it aloud. All three boys ran face-first into the tree, scuffing their foreheads and chins and fingertips, tasting bark and blood.

For a moment, they scurried against each other like mice, and visible somewhere in the upheaval were Willie's stunned eyes, filled with the awareness that he could not join them because of his missing arm, their failure with the pulley, maybe more reasons. Willie would be left behind to be eaten by the truck, or by the man who drove the truck, or by his parents, or by the other people in the world who sooner or later always consumed boys like Willie. He could not fight it.

But then they surged upward, Reggie and James, and somehow, unbelievably, Willie found himself rising. He felt his toes find the almost-forgotten footholds of those plank steps, felt his one hand take hold and help to lift his body heavenward. His friends were all around him, multitudes of them, pushing with arms and legs and shoulders and knees, creating unlikely human slings, fantastic stepping stones, miraculous braces, and somehow Willie continued to rise, up, up, higher and higher. It was something that made no sense, something nearly impossible. Reggie and James scrambled up the tree in a motion like the flex of a single complicated muscle, and through some strange magic, brought Willie up with them.

They collapsed over the edge of the tree house floor. They winced and grunted and pushed Willie inside. Willie rolled over and then came to a halt in a sitting position, his eyes wild, his face flushed, thrilled and mystified by his sudden and unexpected ascent. He was grinning and his eyes were wet.

Immediately the three huddled together. For the first time in hours they could see each other clearly, and even though it was dark they were energized by the strength they saw. Eyes were bright. Chests beat up and down. Sweat glistened from faces and necks. They were scared but alive.

Their breathing slowed. They remembered to blink. Reality began to seep back into their minds. There was no truck. There had never been a truck. It had only been their minds playing. *Playing*. The word was an insult, and they looked away from one other, suddenly uncomfortable.

And then with a squeal, something smashed into the tree.

The boys screamed and their hands went out and they gripped whatever they could. Splinters entered palms. Shoulders jammed painfully into hard corners. What was happening? What was this? They had heard no engine approach.

Yet now, from directly below, came a high-pitched shredding against the base of the tree. Every board of the tree house vibrated and moaned; nails inside each board sang in protest. A smell like smoke and rubber filled the air. The large Mel Herman painting still tacked to the wall—forgotten evidence of Reggie and James's private tree house meetings—wrinkled and nearly tore before once again pulling taut. Willie started mumbling things beneath the engine's throaty groan; strange, complicated sentences with improbable words: "meat," "jokers," "pawn," "devil."

Reggie fell flat to his stomach. He had to see what was down there, he had to know. Willie and James held themselves tight in opposite corners, watching in disbelief as Reggie squirmed forward inch by inch and peeked his head over the far edge of the tree house.

"What?" demanded James.

"Truck," said Reggie, as if only mildly surprised.

Below, cloaked by the steam that poured from its front hood, was a truck, its front end wrapped around the base of the tree. Its wheels were spinning. It was stuck. Then suddenly it dislodged and jumped several yards back. The engine spit violently and then the truck roared and leapt once more.

The world shook. Reggie howled and ducked back into the tree house, covering his face with his hands. Willie and James shouted as the tree branches shook and the tree house itself spun, as if it were screwing loose from the tree. There was a snapping, splintering noise and the boys watched in terror as three floorboards buckled and crumbled into wreckage.

Willie's mumbling continued, his lips moving faster and faster, his sentences flipping inside out until they could not possibly contain meaning, not even to Willie. James thought he heard the word "vacancy" in there, again and again, the piercing stab of the "V" sound cutting through the truck's oceanic thrum, but James did not know if Willie was describing that old motel, this tree house, or himself.

Outside, the screech of a pig being slaughtered—the truck—and then a sound like a thousand lightbulbs stamped beneath a thousand boots. The tree limbs flailed and the tree house twisted. Half of a wall fell away and the boys heard it pound against the ground several seconds later. No longer was the tree house as straight and sharp as an unspoiled grave; now it was as warped as Greg Johnson's resting spot—the roof, the floor, the walls, everything bending and peeling off into a spray of wood chips. Mel Herman's torn and flapping artwork shone through the chaos, the hard slashes of color finally transporting to the real world: here was the violence the paint predicted, *right here*. There was a deafening blast as the long-forgotten metal pulley crashed through the weakened ceiling, the flimsy floor, then vanished.

Through the rattling darkness, Reggie and James found the white flash of each other's eyes. They were both lying flat on the disintegrating floor of the tree house, their mouths stretched wide. They might have been screaming, the both of them, it was impossible to tell. Yet they both realized the same thing at the same time.

Willie was no longer talking.

They twisted their heads to the corner where Willie should have been, his head between knees, his single arm folded across the top of his head. Willie was not there and the entire corner was gone.

Another screaming metal crunch filled their ears and the tree moaned in misery. The tree house soared outward as if it planned to launch itself like a baseball. At the last second the tree snatched it back, and that's when the roof exploded into a shower of wooden daggers that rained upon the boys, scarred their legs, nicked the backs of their necks. Rusty nails landed in their hair; they felt other nails, cold and laden with tetanus beneath the palms of their hysterical hands. Before they shut their eyes they glimpsed the night sky totally exposed above them.

Wait—there was Willie! He had escaped from the collapsed corner and now hobbled like a three-legged dog through the hailstorm of wood. Reggie and James were frozen—without realizing it, they had accepted their fates—yet Willie was moving. His knees shoveled through inches of loose white wood and the colored confetti of Mel Herman's painting as the floor bucked and writhed below him like the back of a giant beast. Willie's face remained focused as he headed toward the widening mouth of the tree house door.

Alone, neither Reggie nor James had the courage to move. They were too scared, too shocked, too small, too powerless. But when they looked past Willie and at each other, there was something between them just strong enough.

James took to his knees and lunged. Reggie rolled his body over the sharp shreds of wood. They were faster than Willie, and in a flash they crossed the undulating floor. They sank their hard fists into Willie's clothes and when Willie felt it he exclaimed—loudly, angrily—and clambered for the doorway with an authority neither of the boys expected. Reggie and James cried and pounced. James swiped for Willie's left arm, the one that wasn't there, and James felt certain that for the rest of his life he would feel the tickle of that ghost arm fluttering through his empty fingers. Willie toppled halfway out the door and dove down at the truck. But Reggie had found a grip and now James found one, too; but then they both felt Willie's shirt ripping, yawning away. So they fell upon Willie's legs and wrapped their arms around them. Willie's torso dangled above the truck.

Willie was shouting something that sounded like *He only wants me!,* and even in the crash and fury of that moment, there was something in Willie's voice that staggered Reggie and James. Willie did not sound scared, he sounded mad, mad at *them.* Willie kicked his legs—at them, at Reggie and James—maybe because Willie wanted them to let him go, let him fall, so that he could finally prove to them his worth.

The tree house convulsed. A huge hole gulped away the center of the floor and Reggie felt one of his legs flop through. He loosened his grip on Willie's pants leg and immediately got an eyeful of Willie's shoe. Reggie reeled away, letting go of Willie to save himself. Willie's body slid out the doorway and James wrapped his arms around Willie's thigh, then his calf, now his foot, desperately clawing and clinging, shouting something, maybe,

Don't go, please Willie don't go! For an instant the world narrowed down: gone were the tree house, the tree, the truck, the noise, the night. The world reduced to two things: James's hands and Willie's left foot.

And then the tree shook and the truck backed up and Willie wriggled and the truck spun its tires and James screamed and the truck lurched ahead and then Willie dropped like a stone, heavy and silent, and James held only a single, tiny tennis shoe that was once worn by a boy named Willie Van Allen.

Good Endings Leave Nothing Definite

People forget things. Even grown-ups, who spend so much energy insisting that they are right, and that they are the only ones who know the correct course to take, even they eventually forget why they are insisting. They get distracted by their jobs, by the monthly bills, by that damn car that keeps breaking down, by that rainstorm, by that snowstorm, by that visit from Grandma, by how fast the kids are growing, like weeds, taller and taller every day. In the dull light of such events, even the hit-and-run killer soon faded into shadow.

It was a tragedy, no doubt. It was on front pages for

weeks. Mr. Van Allen, boiling over with alcohol and consumed with grief and rage over the lifting of the curfew, had finally decided to disassemble the tree house that he himself had assembled, even if it meant smashing the thing to bits with his truck. He never heard over the engine the cries of the children above him, nor did he see his son when he dropped into the truck's path.

What no one noticed was that Mr. Van Allen's blue truck looked silver in the glow of the moon. All summer Mr. Van Allen had tried to bury a nightmare. He dreamt that one day in early April he had forgotten to pick up his son from that stupid junkyard, and so hurried to his truck and drove fast to make up time, but the alcohol fumes rising from his mouth blinded him and scrambled around all of his senses, and he barely noticed when he bounced something small and nearly weightless from the side of the road, then kept on driving.

When he sobered and returned to a changed wife and a son with one less arm, he knew all apologies were inadequate. The truth, in fact, would surely destroy all three of them. Instead he would keep the secret in the hope that it would consume him alone. But his self-destruction was worse than he expected, more prolonged and painful, and he pleaded each day for someone to end the torture and discover what he had done. When he read about the cancellation of the curfew, he knew it meant that his agony was forever—and then he heard about what someone had done to Greg Johnson's grave, the last thing that poor little boy had been given. It could wait no longer, the tree house had to come down; it was an affront to the Johnsons, to anyone who had to look upon the belongings of boys who had stopped existing.

When the grown-ups of the town saw Mr. Van Allen over the next few months—as he was placed into the back of a police car, led to the courthouse, and transferred to the county jail—they tried to tell one another about the tentative, exhausted, penitent smile that loosened his knotted face. The grown-ups tried to communicate this, but they failed because it scared them.

Greg Johnson's killer was never identified, nor was the driver who desecrated Greg's grave. There were rumors, unreliable sightings, supposed newspaper reports of similar patterns of slaughter. As months wore into years, the alleged locations changed, as did the methods of murder. But it was always the same killer, it had to be, for the threat felt identical to the grown-ups, who stirred their drinks with their fingers and used the blare of television to drown out the undying uncertainty. There were also occasional rumors of a quick and bloody justice, of groups of parents tracking the killer and bringing about a reckoning. The grown-ups knew this was only wishful thinking, and besides—there was something about these rumors that made them feel even worse.

This killer would live forever. In fact, he had already lived that long.

Before the police arrived at the scene of the accident, James escaped home and came upon a brightly lit living room. His father was gone—again, he was *always* gone—and his mother was surrounded by wads of tissue as pink and as puffy as her eyes. Her makeup was mostly wiped away and her scar glowed bright like bone. James wondered how she had heard about the tree house so quickly. Then he realized that his mother had her own heartbreak: his missing father. James stood there panting in the corner, unseen and painted with the red hieroglyphics of wood scratches, and in that long moment he vowed to fix the family that lay scattered before him. If his mother and father were indeed too damaged to do anything but harm each other, he would become their emissary and take them proudly where they wanted to go: high school, college, and beyond. All this would be theirs, starting now.

Reggie was escorted home by a police officer. Like Mr. Wahl, Ms. Fielder was gone. Reggie waited in the living room. He turned on the stereo and the television, and turned up both so loud it hurt his ears and vibrated the fillings inside his teeth. Then he got a tub of ice cream and kept eating it, more and more, until it ran down his chin and neck and his entire face was so cold he couldn't cry even if he wanted. Later his mother rushed in the door, her blond ponytail whipping about her shoulders, and when she saw him she stopped suddenly and her face trembled like she was afraid. She opened her arms. *I'm not hugging you,* Reggie thought to himself, the ice cream spoon buried deep inside his mouth. But a few seconds later there he was, across the room, his cold face buried inside the hot, hard folds of his mother's uniform. She pet his head with hands that felt like they belonged to Mom, not to Kay, and said, "Shhh, shhh, shhh," over and over, even though he wasn't making any noise. Reggie wrapped his arms around her skinny hips and told himself he would let go soon. He did not.

* * *

Summer ended.

Months ago, children would've bet money against it. But it happened—it ended just as suddenly as it had arrived. Now it was fall, and the new, cool air cut right through boys' too-thin jackets and chilled their shoulders, shoulders that were a little broader and stronger than before. James and Reggie put on new sneakers and coats and hats and felt strange about how often they forgot Willie, but Reggie's words had ultimately been proven true: there were places they would go that Willie could not follow. After a while, they thought of Willie only when they observed the pack of wild dogs roaming the woods near the old Van Allen place, scrapping for food and overturning trash cans.

On the late autumn day that James's father boxed up his clothes and moved out of the house, James found himself at the vacant junkball diamond. It was not a divorce, not yet, but his parents could no longer live together, even though the relationship between Mr. Wahl and Ms. Fielder had ended. Thinking back on that sweltering day when the three boys had followed Mel

Herman home, it was funny how that shabby motel loomed increasingly large in James's memory while Mel grew increasingly small. James kicked at the damp infield and could taste the dirt, just barely, inside his throat.

For some reason he felt nothing about his parents' separation; he felt as if all his nerve endings had been severed just below the skin. When he returned home from the junkball field he was dreaming about the approaching snow, not his parents, and he had his head thrust deep inside the refrigerator before it hit him. His father was gone. James remained bent over the cold cuts and milk jugs for a long time, the heavy drift of frigid air turning his skin cold and white.

As if to fill the home that suddenly loomed too large, James's mother loved him harder than ever before. She was always there for him, on time, even early. If she had a single unkind thought it did not pass her lips or alter her features. James should have been pleased, but there was something he did not count on. She annoyed him. He didn't know if it was her constant, overeager smile and the fawning way she spooned him second helpings of absolutely everything, or the cautious way that she handled him, both physically and verbally, ever since Willie died. It was as if James was an animal that might bare its teeth or flee if his mother made a single threatening move. He thought about both: biting, running. He also thought something else. Maybe tiring of your mother was just what happened when you grew up.

His father lived in a nice apartment across town and

James saw him regularly. Never once did his father mention the theft of the Monster, nor to James's knowledge did the news ever reach his mother. James was thankful, at least at first. Later, he felt angry that he was obligated to feel thankful. Then he began to wish his father would go ahead and tell on him, to his mother, his teachers, everyone, because until the secret was told James owed his father a loyalty. But his father did nothing, and James did nothing, too, and this uncomfortable, unspoken pact between father and son stretched out, further and further, until it became their lives.

The divorce did come eventually. Alone with his mother, money was not as plentiful as before. Louise, after over a decade with the family, had already been let go. James's mother once again found herself facing the backyard clothesline on windy days, wrestling with laundry, those twisted, anguished cords. Only this time instead of turning to her husband for permission to quit, she turned to her son. James did not feel it was his permission to give and so withheld it.

High school began. James never forgot the chief lesson he had learned the night the tree house came down: he was not breakable. After the death of his friend and the divorce of his parents, he felt deep within him the need to test this theory, to do things liable to injure and scar him. But he honored the vow he had made to his parents and instead kept his mind on the donut, escaping his mother's relentless cheer by immersing himself in tennis, basketball, the drama club, the student newspaper. He volunteered at a nursing home and worked fundraisers for local associations. He met girls and stayed out late, but not too late, even learning how to kiss them. The scrapbook his mother kept, stagnant for so many years, began to thicken.

Reggie was part of none of this. The junkyard fight remained interrupted. When tenth grade began and Reggie was not there, James did not investigate the reason, though he thought about it for months, wondering if Reggie had dropped out, if he still lived with his mother just a few blocks away. In a way, James was glad he was gone. Forgetting the summer of his twelfth year was already a goal nearly achieved, and seeing Reggie's face in the crowd had only made that goal more elusive.

Yet even as he was nominated to the homecoming court, made the all-state track team, graduated at the head of his class, and started to pack for college, James still longed for the danger of his childhood summers, those days of rushing through scrap heaps and thorns, those nights of broken curfews and cheated deaths. With peril now kept at such a distance, each day that passed was a mere drop of blood from a wound that, though mortal, would take a lifetime to drain.

Sometimes James's eyes would open in the middle of the night and he would lie there, caught in a dream vision of Willie. It was always the same. There he was, helping Willie limp away from the junkyard, Willie weighing little more than a laundry bag filled with old bones. As the memory took him, dozens of Willie's nonsense sentences whispered in his ears, and he wished that someone would write them down in memory of Willie, because soon they would be forgotten. In the violet shushing of night, none of this disturbed him. He believed that he had been a good friend to Willie. Maybe a best friend. He was glad.

* * *

The day after Willie's funeral, Reggie's mother threw some stuff in the back of the car and they took a vacation, the two of them, their first one ever. Without makeup, her hair flying free, Reggie's mother drove with her right leg pushing the gas pedal and her left propped acrobatically against the dash. With no destination in mind they drove for nearly two hours without a word, perhaps because the wind blasting through the open windows made conversation impossible, or perhaps because his mother's mouth was too busy beckoning the ashes of one cigarette after another.

Around noon they pulled off at a roadside diner. His mother walked inside and Reggie followed. They sat in a booth. Music jangled loudly from a jukebox. Even louder, the hiss of a grill. Reggie stared at his menu and felt as if, once more, he was being held inside for recess until he could complete a difficult assignment—the menu was all letters and numbers and none of it added up. He stole a look at his mother and she was glaring at him.

"You want the burger," she said. "Mustard, mayo, pickle on the side."

A waitress appeared. His mother recited their choices with brusque authority. Reggie tried not to watch but was spellbound. He soon realized why. He was at a restaurant with his mother and *she was not the waitress*. She was the one sitting down. She was the one giving her order. Later, as he gnashed his pink hamburger and sucked down the limp yellow pickle, he watched his mother complain about cold onion rings and receive steaming hot replacements, he watched her demand not two coffee refills but three, he watched her slap down money for the bill and send a tip skittering across the flyspecked tabletop.

She drained her cup and sized up Reggie over the rim. The stillness of her unpainted eyes, her chipped and bitten nails, the disarray of her blond hair: she was so tough, and he so small. Reggie felt a stubborn thickening of his chest. He flattened his bottom lip and squared his jaw. Two could play at this game. He was tough, just as tough; she was nothing he couldn't become. And so they sat there and frowned, enduring corny jukebox harmonies and the high-pitched exasperation of the grill.

"Finish your fries," she grunted at last.

"I'm finished," he grunted back. She considered this for a moment, then sat taller. He sat taller, too, propping a leg beneath himself for the boost. A puff of air flared her nostrils. She palmed her smokes and got up. Outside, on the way back to the car, she smacked the back of Reggie's head; without hesitating Reggie twisted a leg and booted his mother in the rear. They did not look at one another when they sat down in the car, but both had the feeling that the other was concealing a grin. They were worthy rivals, the two of them. They knew it and relished the challenge.

Their trip together lasted half a lifetime, even more. Or so it seemed when Reggie thought about it three years later, when his mother moved both of them into the home of her newest boyfriend, Darren. Reggie wondered how it had happened—he had promised himself he would not go through this again. Yet when the moving day came, he did not run away. He helped his mother pack and they moved, this time thirty minutes away and into a different school system.

He had to make new friends, which wasn't much fun, and he had to accustom himself to another new house as well as another fake dad with his own unpredictable smells and habits and rules. Reggie had to admit that Darren treated Kay decently, or at least better than his predecessors had treated her. It was not long before she took a job tending bar down the street from the gas station where Darren worked; they often met for lunch. Sometimes Reggie joined them, because he too was working at the garage. The first morning Reggie had woken up in Darren's house, Darren had marched him down to the garage and told the boss, Gerald, to hire him. Reggie was handed a pair of overalls. He began to foment a new plan of escape.

Then something unexpected happened. One day while hammering metal, changing tires, and persuading bolts into sockets, Reggie found something he was not looking for: pride. He was good at fixing cars. No, he was better than good. He was the best mechanic in the whole garage, and he was only a kid. His fantasies of flight–hitching a ride down South, joining the military, going wherever the nearest railcar would take him–soon fell from his mind. He was exactly where he should be.

The age difference between him and his mother flattened and disappeared. They became more like roommates than mother and son; she was more Kay to him now than Mom. By the time he was a senior, it felt as if he had overtaken her in age and that he was the parent, she the child. He had to remind her of her shifts at the bar. He had to tell her when she let Darren get away with too much bullshit. Sometimes the phone would ring in the early morning and it would be Gerald saying that someone was calling in sick and they needed Reggie down there pronto. And Reggie would get up, pull on his overalls, and bang on his mother's door to make sure she woke up on time. As he walked to the garage he didn't think to himself how grown-up he was acting. Instead he thought that he owed this much to Kay, because if he turned out all right she might believe she had been an all right mother. Stepping into the familiar coolness of the garage, Reggie remembered the junkball plays Mel Herman had tried to teach, and recalled that the hit-and-run rarely worked but the sacrifice fly was possible if you just concentrated.

Reggie graduated from high school with a C average, but found something better than high marks: Addie, a girl he met one day at the garage. She was perfect, much better than he deserved, and once he had her he did not let her leave his side. That was easy, because she didn't want to.

He told Addie about Willie Van Allen. She was the first and only person he'd ever told. Had he been able to predict Willie's death, he told her, he would've guessed that it would toughen him up, make him more like the older kids he had idolized and finally become. Instead, remembering Willie dragged Reggie back to those days when he was smaller and weaker. For a long time, he had hated Willie for that.

But after they moved in with Darren, recollections of Willie's sincerity and gratitude stopped Reggie from landing in more trouble. He *wouldn't* push that kid into his locker. He *wouldn't* sass Gerald to his face. Reggie would walk away from these near-incidents with fists trembling and a love for Willie Van Allen flickering white hot in his gut, his eyes, his ears—he could feel Willie alive all over his skin. Reggie never thanked Willie for these interventions, at least not out loud. However, the way in which he protected the memory of that sickly looking, long-nosed, one-armed, brace-faced, forever-young little boy was, to say the least, very out of character for him—and both he and Addie knew it. Allowing Willie to forever hide away inside his head . . . well, it wasn't much. Reggie still hoped it was worth something.

* * *

One week after Willie Van Allen's death, school started up. Mel Herman was not there. There were theories, each wilder and more haunting than the last. Finally a rumor went around that Mr. Camper, the art teacher, knew what had happened to Mel. When asked, Mr. Camper was shruggy and mumbly, almost as if he had been sworn to silence. A few kids, however, claimed that if you really searched among that long hair, beard, and pilled flannel collars, there was a clue—look there, can't you see it? Mr. Camper is *smiling*.

What do you do when a lifelong threat disappears all at once? The kids did not know and did not relish finding out. With Mel Herman gone, they felt more vulnerable than ever—now there was no telling where to look for life's next attack. So they spoke of Mel the way the grown-ups spoke of the hit-and-run killer, as something mythic and dreadful that would return the very day they relaxed their guard. Over the summer someone had stolen the Mel Herman paintings that had formerly lined the school hallways. There was nothing left to challenge his boogeyman status.

Mel did in fact leave one thing behind, though very few ever saw it. That winter, when the coroners came to remove Miss Bosch, who had passed away silently during the night, they found her lying within the most spectacularly painted bedroom they had ever seen. Scab reds, sweat yellows, bruise purples, leather blacks, latchkey golds, sidewalk grays, road-sign oranges, dollar-bill greens, medicine-bottle tans, poached-egg whites, oxygen-tank blues, baseball-bat browns, girlie-mag pinks, knife-blade silvers: it was mesmerizing, and the coroners fell to the floor twisting their necks. As they lifted Miss Bosch from her bed they remarked that they kept expecting her eyes to shoot open, for a nest of such colors made it seem nearly impossible for the woman to be dead.

Mel came back to town when the arts academy let out at Christmas, and his father's new nurse met him at the door with a cry of delight. Her name was Louise, and she was the unexpected result of an anxious phone call Mel had placed to the community hospital the night before he had taken a bus to the city. "My dad needs help," he had said, and after ascertaining that there was no immediate medical emergency, the man on the phone had assisted him, made a few calls, and found a wonderful woman who had recently lost her job and was looking for just this kind of work.

Louise was nothing like Mel was expecting and like no one he had met before. She laughed like a storm siren and tore around the house crying this and demanding that, throwing open drapes and chucking musty stacks of paper into the trash. When Mel sloped past her on his way in the front door, she told him he stank—hit the showers and make it quick because there's turkey roasting in the oven. As she snapped and chuckled and thundered through the narrow hallways, Mel's father snorted and groused. "You're going to kill me," he muttered to her with a trace of a smile. A smile—on his father's face! Mel panicked and dove into the shower.

Why had it not occurred to him earlier that help like Louise was available? Mel thought about it as hot water covered him and realized that sometimes big changes, like going away to school, shook up not only your life but the lives of everyone around you. Those changes could be good or bad, but you'd never know unless you started shaking.

It was a strange dinner, consisting of foods Mel could not believe his father would eat. But he did, after muttering plenty of halfhearted complaints. Louise did all the talking while Mel and his father scrutinized one another, their faces flexing over mouthfuls of turkey. "Your dad wants to know if you've seen your brother," Louise said. Mel kept chewing, shook his head. "Well, will you let us know if you see him? Your dad talks about him more than you would believe." It was an easy request to grant. Mel thought about his brother constantly, and clung to a dream that one day his brother would hear a rumor about a student at the arts academy so talented you had to see him to believe, and at that moment his brother would know it just had to be Mel.

Mel kept chewing, nodded. "I'll let you know," he answered.

Late that night Mel crept into his brother's room and placed the switchblade back where nearly a year ago he had found it. Almost at once, his chest ached. But in the city, at the academy, where paint flowed so fast that it swept sudden, uncertain friendships along in its startling tide, he was afraid a heart of metal would make him sink.

Walking back to the bus station on New Year's Eve, Mel Herman was the only one in town to see Mrs. Van Allen pack up and leave town. Mel paused beneath a tree just down the street, snowflakes thickening his lashes and melting into his blinking eyes, and he watched the stocky woman struggle to lift scores of boxes and suitcases into the back of a rental trailer. Mel thought of helping her, maybe without even asking for money, but he could not make his cold bones move. Mrs. Van Allen went from the house to the trailer, over and over again. Her silver hair was dyed brown and done up nice, but the steady snowfall pounded it.

Mel hitched up his bag; he had a bus to catch. For a strange moment he imagined that he was Willie Van Allen, hitching up his own bag with just one arm and leaving his parents forever. Mel looked up at a tall tree as he passed and thought he saw tree house boards still nailed to faraway limbs.

Sometimes it's okay to run, he whispered to Mrs. Van Allen as he shambled his way past the house, but the words swept up and away, became snow.

NOW

Run

T hump thump thump–

When the gasoline stopped gushing and the nozzle hiccupped and shuddered inside the tank, both James and Reggie blinked. The air, so clear there for a moment, was again marred with the clatter from the garage, the ticking of the other pumps, and the rasp of truck tires, newly heavy with petroleum, peeling from the dirty cement. The two little boys again had escaped from their father and were weaving circles around the grown-ups, around James and Reggie, around everything.

"Yeah," answered James. "I remember almost everything."

Reggie lifted the nozzle from the tank and returned it to its rusted housing in a motion so practiced James found it nearly miraculous. Reggie was not just bigger, he was better, his wounds deeper, his willpower stronger. He no longer seemed like a troubled kid heading for the same prison cell as his father, nor would he drink away his years in the same bar where his mother wiped up after local farmhands. There had been violence in Reggie's past, but there had been just enough goodness, too, and the result was the man that now stood before James, almost fully formed.

"You always had a pretty good memory, I guess," said Reggie, looking toward the garage as if itching to get back in there and put his hands to metal. James thought of the months following Willie's death, before Reggie moved away, and how on occasion the two of them would still laugh together about things: Mel Herman, Reggie's mom, even the divorce that split up James's parents. It felt good to laugh at those things, and then ignore them because they meant so little—or so much that they were best forgotten. Then even ignoring these things became a chore, and each time the two boys saw each other they would have to grin bigger and laugh harder than before. Eventually they began avoiding each other, pretending not to notice as they passed on different sides of the same street. There was an expanding world to explore, and their exchanges just took too much energy. By the time of their last interaction in the boys' room at the end of ninth grade, they barely recognized one another, and could only hazily recall the time when they saved each other's lives almost daily. Thinking of it now filled James with so much shame he felt like running, and when he looked at his car packed with college supplies he realized that was exactly what he was doing.

It had to stop; he had done too much running already. He wasn't like his parents, he couldn't be, and only Reggie had the power to wrestle him back to the kind of boy who took on any fight that crossed his path without regard to pain. Like Reggie, he was now bigger, but was he any better? He thought about all of his high school accomplishments, packed neatly in boxes back at home, and decided that, no, he was no better than he had been at twelve. In fact, perhaps his one chance at greatness had slipped away the same moment he gave up Reggie's Monster, the only unique thing he had ever possessed. All at once he felt the Monster's absence as deeply as someone else would feel a missing arm, and he wanted it back, all of it—the Monster, Reggie, Willie, everything.

Reggie looked again at the garage. Anxiety engulfed James. The fight was slipping away yet again, he could feel it. Everyone had their scars, most of all Reggie, and though James had tried to wound himself by shrugging off his current life as carelessly as possible, it had not worked. He was still clean and untouched. In a moment, Reggie would walk away, and selfishly he would take the fight with him.

"Hit me," James said.

Reggie wiped his nose, squinted.

James spoke again. "I said hit me."

A smile crept over Reggie's face, but it broke halfway. A thrill of excitement spread through James's chest: for once the advantage was his.

"Why would I want to do that?" Reggie asked slowly. The half grin remained but his eyes were cautious and alight.

James saw pictures: green bruises, hanging scabs, bloody teeth. "You have to," he said. "This is our last chance."

The smile, if that's what it was, drained from Reggie's face. He looked down at his arms, saw the nicks of blood sparkling through clotted grease. He raised his hands and gazed at both sides, as if shocked by how large they were, how threatening. He too seemed to realize it: the time was now, the characters were present, and the setting was right—encroached on all sides by wrecked cars, the gas station made a suitable substitute for the junkyard. James took in air, kept it. He tensed his muscles, set his jaw for violence, and readied himself to retaliate.

The dangerous things that were Reggie's hands glided back down to his sides. James suspected trickery; he inhaled even more deeply; black spots danced before his eyes. But there was no cruelty in Reggie's face, only patience.

"You're not going to prison, James," he said. "Things are going to be okay."

James's shoulders–they were shaking. He could not help it. There was liquid in his eyes. He blinked and some of it fell. He was eighteen, not twelve, but once again fought back tears. He was back at Greg Johnson's funeral, Willie Van Allen's wake, straining to keep himself together and finding the needed strength from the one person who always stood with him: Reggie.

Strength was still the offer and James, his vision a blur, reached out and took it. It turned out to be Reggie's hand, and he was shaking it, and the sweat mixed with his own, palm to palm, blood brothers once more.

And then they were apart and it was over. Words were still coming, but it was only conversation, the niceties of two grown-ups who ran into each other at the local filling station.

"You still seeing that girl? Betty, Betsy? What was her name?"

"No," James said, sniffing, wiping at his eyes. "You?"

Reggie nodded, happy. "Addie. I wish you could meet her. We're going to get a place. I'm going to open my own garage. Next year, or the one after that. Addie, she wants to have a baby."

"Already?"

"Man, what's already? I don't have time to wait for already. Already is now." Reggie laughed. "My mom sees it a little different, of course. But that's old people for you. They always think everything is their fault."

"It is."

"No, it's us," said Reggie, gently. "We did this to us."

The two little boys roared through, dodging past James, thumping Reggie's hip, leaping over the front bumper of the car and speeding onward, all feet. James and Reggie watched the boys take the corner of the station, their hands scratching like they wanted to murder each other—believable if not for the laughter.

"I *am* going to visit Willie," Reggie said. "I mean it."

"Okay," said James.

"Just remind me where he is."

"Near the back." James rubbed his hands together, watched Reggie's grime disappear into his flesh. It hurt to speak of Willie and look at Reggie, and to wonder if the blood the three friends had shared still beat in rhythm somewhere inside their estranged bodies. "Maybe three rows from the back. His gravestone is pretty small. But you'll find it."

In that last moment, the shouts of the two little boys still dying in his ears, James wondered which of the two of them—he or Reggie—would live to see the other buried, and if he, whoever he was, would need to ask around to locate the plot. For the first time, James saw an upside to being tied to Reggie Fielder, an advantage every bit as powerful as being tied to Willie Van Allen. Being connected in such a way was like being given a rare glimpse of the future—you knew, in part, where you were headed. Weight that had been upon James's shoulders for longer than he could remember slid away.

Reggie slapped the pump. "Look, this tank's on me." He felt around for his rag, saw that it still lay atop James's car, and so wiped his hands on his overalls, nodding slowly and backing away. "You'll do good, James. Don't you worry."

Then there was a shout—"Fielder!"—from inside the garage, and Reggie's face softened with relief. He grinned at James, winked, and sprinted. Without turning around or saying goodbye, Reggie Fielder hurried into the garage and melted into darkness.

James opened the car door, sat down, and steadied his hands on the wheel. The fight was not over, but at least it was his to win or lose on his own. He stared at the graduation tassel, which hung motionless. Maybe Reggie was right. Maybe he *could* do good.

He turned the key. The car, filled with gasoline from the most important gas station in the world, roared to life. James put the vehicle into gear and pulled forward, making sure the two little boys were out of the way. He looked into his rearview mirror, finally not noticing the tassel, and watched Reggie's stained cloth slide down the car's back window and fall away.

James brought the car around. The tires settled as they found the smoother surface of the highway. He felt a smile touch his face. He knew where he was headed.

DANIEL KRAUS is a writer, editor, and filmmaker. He lives with his wife in Chicago. Visit him at www.danielkraus.com.